THE PACT OF THE WOLVES

THE PACT OF THE WOLVES

NINA BLAZON

TRANSLATED BY SUE INNES

Text © 2008 Nina Blazon
English language translation © Sue Innes, 2008

Annick Press Ltd.

Original title: Der Bund der Wölfe, by Nina Blazon
© 2006, Patmos Verlag GmbH & Co. KG, Sauerländer Verlag, Düsseldorf

All rights reserved. No part of this work covered by the copyrights hereon may be reproduced or used in any form or by any means—graphic, electronic, or mechanical—without prior written permission of the publisher.

Copy edited by Tanya Trafford
Cover design by Ellie Exarchos
Interior design by Lisa Hemingway
Cover photos: (woman's torso) © Brad Wilson/Photonica/Getty Images; (wolf head) © istockphoto.com

Cataloguing in Publication
Blazon, Nina, 1969–
The pact of the wolves / Nina Blazon ; translated by Sue Innes.

Translation of: Der Bund der Wölfe.
ISBN 978-1-55451-124-2 (bound)
ISBN 978-1-55451-135-8 (pbk.)

I. Innes, Susan J. II. Title.
PT2662.L298B8613 2008 J833'.92 C2007-906823-5

We acknowledge the support of the the Book Publishing Industry Development Program (BPIDP) for our publishing activities. We further acknowledge the support of the Canada Council for the Arts.

The publication of this work was supported by a grant from the Goethe-Institut.

Printed and bound in Canada.

Published in the U.S.A. by
Annick Press (U.S.) Ltd.

Distributed in Canada by
Firefly Books Ltd.
66 Leek Crescent
Richmond Hill, ON
L4B 1H1

Distributed in the U.S.A. by
Firefly Books (U.S.) Inc.
P.O. Box 1338
Ellicott Station
Buffalo, NY 14205

Visit our website at **www.annickpress.com**

CONTENTS

PROLOGUE

SINCE BEFORE THE BEGINNING of time It had been creeping through the passageways. The place was dark as night, but Its eyes were aware of every shadow in every corner, every crack between the stone slabs of the floor. It could discern every odor—odors that alternated between old dust and a new, unfamiliar smell. Again and again It had tried to stand upright, only to end up making Its way, as usual, on all fours.

Even the sound-making Being running ahead of It on two legs seemed to have realized that even though It was crawling, It was faster, much faster, than the Being itself, which was apparently unable to see well in the darkness. Painstakingly, the Being felt its way along the walls, stumbling occasionally, each time giving out sounds of fury.

Keeping time with Its gasping breaths, Its claws clicked over the stone, which suddenly no longer felt rough and cold, but unusually smooth. Around Its body the space expanded to a boundlessness that chilled It to the marrow. From one moment to the next It seemed to be floating in nothingness, or in one of those dreams that so often haunted It. When It slept, Its world would fragment into colors, images, and grotesque faces, until

It started up in terror, Its claws hurting, because in Its dream world It had clawed into iron. It would smell blood and awake in the musty scent of Its familiar low-ceilinged den, where It dozed away Its days. Claw marks lined the gray walls all around It.

And yet this boundless place did not seem to be an illusion. It could not understand the pleasant sounds that the Being had made, but some were familiar and made It feel good. The Being still ran ahead, bent over—they were now moving so fast that It seemed to fly over the smooth floor, intoxicated by all that space. The world smelled different here—strangely sharp—and all the sounds were bright. When It bent down and ran Its nose over the smooth ground, the Being called to It .

"Come!" urged the Being. It knew this word well, but from the mouth of the strange Being it did not sound like an order, but rather a caress. "Come, please, come with me!" the voice entreated, and suddenly the Being came back and bent down to It, its embrace wrapping itself around It. It felt the Being's dread, took it up into Itself until Its muscles began to tremble and It closed Its eyes with fear. Garish, strange images bombarded It. Even so, It let Itself be pulled upright. It snarled, because being touched was an unfamiliar sensation—maybe even dangerous. Swaying and bent over, It stood there and leaned on the Being, feeling its racing heart.

"Come with me!" the Being repeated. The smell of skin rose into Its nose, pleasant and strangely familiar. It dropped to the ground again. Whispered, incomprehensible sounds penetrated Its consciousness. But the Being did not seem to hear the creeping and shuffling, now getting louder and louder. Light flickered over floor and walls. The Being cried out, and It crawled backwards, so quickly that It bumped into something transparent, hard, and gave a howl of pain. A voice boomed;

there were shouts, footsteps. Something brushed along Its shoulder. For the first time in Its life, It snapped at a hand, but Its teeth sank into air, for in the light It was blind. A dull thud, as a shape seized the Being and threw it to the ground. Sounds of pain and sharp words flew back and forth, and somebody shouted at the Being, which, like It, was cowering on the ground. The Being shouted something too, and then there was another thud.

"Come!" That word again, this time an order. Hissing, It bared Its teeth. Its eyes stung from the blinding light that flitted over the ground, flicked over the smooth transparent object, then shone directly on It. It turned Its head and fled. The next moment Its world shattered in pain. Teeth buried themselves in Its neck and shoulder. The Being cried out one last time. The smell of blood enveloped It. Then all was silent.

BIANCA

BIANCA WAS FREEZING. Although it was the middle of April, she had not brought a jacket. She had expected to be constantly moving, not waiting around like this in the farthest corner of the lawn on the edge of the forest. The school was an angular silhouette against the night sky. A semicircle of torches set on iron stakes lit up the trees behind her.

Two masked figures in dark cloaks carrying torches had just appeared and had taken a second group of students away with them. Now there were just four of them left—two other girls, who had already paired up, and, standing a bit apart from them, Bianca and a lanky boy with short, mousy-brown hair, someone she hadn't noticed this morning at the welcoming ceremony.

"Looks as though they're being led away to their execution, doesn't it?" the lanky boy said, tugging at the zipper of his fleece jacket.

Bianca wrapped her arms around herself and watched the little procession until all she could see was dancing points of light. The last thing she wanted was a conversation. It had to be past midnight and she was exhausted. Memories of the last couple of days ran through her head: the long train ride, the welcoming ceremony, spending her first night alone in her new room in the girls' dormitory wing of the Europa International School.

"If things continue like this, we'll still be standing here tomorrow morning," the boy commented, trying to get the conversation going again. "If I'd known we'd be freezing our butts off like this, I'd have arrived a day later."

The torchlights faded into the distance. "The guy who showed us our rooms today said the "tour" goes to the orphans' cemetery," the boy went on. "The old forest cemetery that used to belong to the convent." Nervously, he fiddled with his jacket again. "I bet a couple of the idiots will jump out from behind the tombstones and yell 'Boo!' And then there's the stupid costumes. It's all so lame."

Bianca looked at the school building again, trying to imagine the convent that had stood there a few centuries ago, instead of the existing modern, flat-roofed building with its many windows. She'd seen an old drawing of the original building in the brochure. The only reminders now of the history of this place were the old orphans' cemetery with the Belverina Chapel, and the exhibits in the Convent Museum. And, of course, all that talk of the pseudo-medieval "Society of Wolves," to which only older students could belong. Kid stuff, thought Bianca.

"What subject are you specializing in?" asked the boy.

"Math—probability and statistics."

"Oh, so you *can* speak." He gave a lopsided grin. "I've registered for the advanced art course. By the way, my name's Jan."

"Oh."

"Am I bothering you?"

"What makes you think that?" she snapped. Even as Bianca spoke, she regretted her rudeness. Ever since her birthday, that cursed sixteenth birthday when everything had gone wrong that could possibly go wrong in her life, she seemed to have forgotten how to talk to other people. Jan immediately fell silent and pretended to study the trees. The two girls moved a little further away so they could text without interruption. Another half hour went by in silence before the points of light began to dance again.

Five figures were coming over the lawn towards them. Two were wearing wolf masks, and the others wore costumes reminiscent of the Middle Ages. One of them glittered bright yellow and red in the torchlight.

"Why are there so many now?" whispered Jan.

"Four to hold us down and one to swing the ax," replied Bianca.

Jan let out a nervous laugh. "It may seem funny now, but on the way here I met a university student—he used to go to school here. He told me something about the Wolves that wasn't so funny."

"Well, clearly he survived the night tour."

"He didn't mention this masquerade. He just said that the Wolves were all freaks and that I should watch out for myself. They dragged a guy who had messed with them out of his room one night, put him in a sack, and threw him into the river."

"What?"

"I'm sure he wasn't exaggerating." Jan lowered his voice to a whisper, as if worried the approaching figures would hear him. "It turned out the sack was easy to open, and the river was only four or five feet deep at that point, but still..."

Bianca shivered. The night seemed even colder. "What happened then?"

"He couldn't prove the Wolves had done anything. They all had alibis, and the headmaster at the time believed them."

"Relax," said Bianca. "It's only a tour—in the brochure they make it sound like a tourist attraction. Once around the campus, to the old manor house, and to the cemetery, that's all."

"Silence! No talking!"

Bianca and Jan spun around. Pointed fangs shone in the torchlight, and empty eye sockets glared at them. A tall, wiry boy in a wolf mask stepped up to them. He carried a spear in one hand and his fur cloak was shabby and smelly, as if it had been in a damp cellar for a long time. From his attitude, Bianca sensed that he was the leader of this masquerade. Another masked figure, wearing a dark-green priest's robe and an iron mask, had come out of the forest too and now stood beside him. Bianca bit back a disparaging comment—their eerie entrance had had its effect and she wasn't feeling quite so bold. How long had these two been lurking in the forest behind them? By this time the others had crossed the lawn and they now formed a circle around the four of them.

"Who shall we take next?" growled the one in the brightly colored robes. From his belt hung what looked like a long, light-colored bone in which holes had been bored at regular intervals. It might have been a flute. There was a jingling sound as he sprang forward and gave Bianca a rough shove.

"Hey!" she cried in protest, taking a step backward. She felt the breath of another of the masked figures on the back of her neck and quickly turned. She looked into dark, almond-shaped eyes.

"Hmm, we'll take those two in the back and this little one," declared one of them. "He'll be scared otherwise, all alone in the dark!" It was a female voice, and her costume was modeled on a nun's habit, except for the large stick she repeatedly slapped into her hand. Bianca remembered something. Could she be the short-haired girl who had assigned them their rooms? Around the chalk-white mask, which gave her face a severe expression, some dark strands poked out. "So, you back there—and you!" thundered the boy who had jostled Bianca, pointing his bone flute at the girls and Jan. As if on command, the others tipped their heads back and started howling, tightening the circle and lifting their torches threateningly.

"Cool it," grumbled Jan. He adjusted his jacket again and joined the two girls. The circle disappeared as two of the Wolves took their places to the right and left of them. They nodded to the others and marched off with the three newbies across the lawn toward the school. Jan looked back and hesitated for a moment, but when he saw Bianca reaching for her bag as if to join the group, he turned around and caught up with the others.

"Where do you think you're going?" asked the nun menacingly, stepping in front of Bianca.

Slap, slap went the stick. "We can't take more than three per tour." Before Bianca could answer, the others had formed a barrier in front of her. Involuntarily, she clung to her bag. The tall boy, the one with the spear, stepped out of the line and paced a circle around her.

"Not so much fun being out here alone, is it?" he murmured. The others laughed, as if on command.

"What do you think you're doing?" asked Bianca indignantly, her voice a little squeakier than she would have liked.

The ringleader stretched out his hand to stroke her black hair. "A genuine Snow White!" he jeered. Dark eyes shone behind his wolf mask. His voice seemed familiar to Bianca...

"I know you," she said. "This afternoon you took us through the school. You're Joaquim."

"Here I'm just one thing—your nightmare..." He paused for effect, "Bianca."

"I'm impressed," she replied mockingly. "Did it take you long to learn all ten new names by heart?"

"We know a lot more about you," whispered Joaquim. "You come from a dinky little town this side of nowhere, read too many detective stories, and want to take psychology at university. You're good at math—but not good enough for this school. And when we've finished with you, you'll understand why."

From the throbbing in her fingers Bianca realized how tightly she had been gripping the straps of her bag. The Wolves were silent now—just a wall of mouths, patches of shadow, and tongues of flame. They inched closer. The nun gripped her stick fiercely. Bianca forced herself to respond calmly.

"Unbelievable," she said to Joaquim, looking him squarely in the face. "You can even read the room assignment lists. When you're all done with your little charade, can we finally get going? No one answered. The silence was suffocating. Then the nun brought up her stick, let out a war cry, and leaped forward. The stick shot out so fast that Bianca hardly had time to react. The weapon stopped directly in front of her nose.

"Broken nose," whispered the nun. Quick as lightning she took another swing and forced Bianca to one side with a feigned blow. "Rib!" The other Wolves laughed. Bianca's heart was racing, and her knees felt as though they were made of rubber. This was no longer a joke.

"Are you scared?" whispered the boy with the bone flute. "You should be!"

Bianca gulped. "Five against one," she replied. "Apparently you're the ones who are scared." The nun sniggered.

Joaquim stepped forward. "Well, we'll see how brave you really are." At a signal from him, his followers took the torches from their stakes. They left only one in place.

"We'll come back," he said quietly. "And we expect you to be here. Or are you going to run straight home to Mommy?"

He laughed, turned around, and walked away. Obediently the rest of the Wolves followed him.

"Ten minutes, Joaquim!" called Bianca after them. "I won't wait any longer than that!"

No one turned around.

Bianca sank down onto the cool grass and tried to breathe calmly. It took her quite a while. Not until the Wolves were long out of sight did she begin to feel angry. Why had she let them intimidate her? Clearly, frightening the new students was part of the program. Well, these dress-up freaks would have a tough time of it with her. She wrapped her arms around her legs and laid her head on her knees. As soon as she shut her eyes, she saw her parents' faces. Just yesterday they had taken her to the station. Through the train window she had watched their unhappy, anxious faces getting smaller and smaller. In some ways, it seemed like years ago, but the feeling of loss was still raw.

When Bianca opened her eyes, she saw only darkness. She must have nodded off. The single torch had gone out, it was even colder and her legs had gone to sleep. Dazed, she rubbed her eyes, groped for her bag, and pulled her watch from the side pocket. The crescent moon was partly obscured by light cloud, and in its weak light she could only guess at the position of the watch hands. She had been alone for nearly an hour. Bianca fought against the impulse to howl with rage. The Wolves had simply left her behind! How could she have been so stupid as to wait at the edge of the forest like a well-trained puppy? She hadn't even been surprised when they had taken the torches with them. Of course: they play this trick on the last student, and today that happened to be her. Slowly she stood up and rubbed her stiff knees.

"Idiots!" she snapped. With halting steps she crossed the lawn, heading for the barely discernable buildings. The bushes seemed like shadowy figures lurking at the side of the main path, but the crunch of shoes on gravel was comforting. Finally, Bianca reached the visitors' parking lot and ran across the paved path towards the main gate.

Directly in front of her stood the old manor house, which had been built at the beginning of the century. Today it served as the boys' dorm. Bianca remembered that the girls' dorm was to the right of the manor house, in the same building as the library, and she headed toward the glass structure. The gate was shut—of course. Looking around, Bianca discovered a side entrance on the left, where the bell and the intercom were. She would have to wake someone up to get inside the building. The sensor light came on automatically, startling her. Bianca hesitated, then rang the bell. Expecting a tired, expressionless voice on the other end, she leaned against the door—and nearly fell face first over the threshold. She peered, dumbfounded, into the dark passageway that lay open before her. The door was open! No voice came over the intercom. Well, at least she would be spared the embarrassment of having to explain what she was doing out here at two in the morning.

The passageway led past the cloakrooms to the entrance hall of the library. The glass doors gleamed, black as swamp water. Here, on safe ground, Bianca felt her exhaustion returning. She just wanted to sleep. She felt a draft on her neck. Somewhere around here there must be an open door or window. Bianca stopped and strained her ears in the darkness. Of course she could hear something—everyone heard noises in the dark.

This one reminded her of a distant metallic whine. Bianca held her breath and waited. The noise stopped, and in its place she thought she sensed a shadowy movement to her right.

"Hello?" she called out tentatively. Silence. Surely the light switch must be somewhere near the doors. She bumped her hand against the hard surface, which was closer than she had expected. Her fingers first touched cold glass, then metal, and, finally, smooth wallpaper. At last she found the switch. Fluorescent light flickered on. Reading tables gleamed among deserted chairs.

Bianca heaved a sigh of relief, made her way past the tables, and darted toward the stairs that led to the second floor. If she remembered correctly, the main room of the library was to the right, and to the left were the stairs leading to the dorm.

As she ran, she almost didn't notice the object on the floor—a rumpled coat of some sort. It looked like someone had just flung it down carelessly. But was there something wrapped up in it? Bianca stopped for a closer look. She noticed fingers poking out from one of the wide sleeves. And half-hidden beneath the turned-down collar, surrounded by dark-gray hair, a cheek was nestled against the stone floor. With an expression of mild amazement, blue, wide-open eyes stared into emptiness.

MADAME LALONDE

MARIE-CLAIRE LALONDE had the situation under control. The headmistress had directed the young detective to seat himself in the chair nearest her desk, kindly, but so firmly that no objection was possible. The sunlight streaming into the room through the high window was blinding. Every time the detective looked up from his notebook to ask Bianca the next question, he squinted. Bianca, on the other hand, was sitting in the shaded corner near the door. The armchair was a little too low to be comfortable. The room itself had an air of serious discussions and important decisions. Normally just students would be sitting here, getting a dressing-down from Madame Lalonde. After a sleepless night, Bianca was feeling unfocused and off balance, but at least she was no longer so cold, now that Madame had pressed a cup of tea into her hands. The detective did not look much more awake.

"All right," he said finally, putting his pen into his breast pocket. "I think that's enough for now." With some effort, he pulled a crumpled card from his well-thumbed datebook. "Here's my contact information." The chair creaked as he leaned toward Bianca.

"Thank you," said Madame Lalonde, quickly intercepting and taking the card in Bianca's place. The detective frowned, but made no objection. For the first time, Bianca thought she saw a flicker of emotion on his face. It seemed clear that he did not particularly care for Madame Lalonde. The headmistress did not sit down at her desk again but remained standing, the card still in her hand. Bianca actually felt grateful at that moment for the commanding manner of this tall, striking woman. The detective stood up.

"If you think of anything else, give me a call," he said, looking directly at Bianca. "Colin Sinclair—it's all on your card." At the word "your," which he stressed, he gave a sidelong glance at the headmistress.

"I will," Bianca managed to say. "Thanks."

"Well then, I should go."

When he offered his hand to shake—a hand that poked out of a wide sleeve a little too long—her stomach lurched. She had to force herself to take it and say goodbye. Madame Lalonde was watching the detective's every move intently—as if she was afraid that he might pull out his gun and carry Bianca off. The door clicked shut, and it was over. Bianca heaved a sigh of relief and slid down deeper into her chair. Her fingers were throbbing from the heat of the cup.

"Drink a little more, at least," said Madame Lalonde. She moved to where the police officer had been sitting. Unlike him, she did not squint, although the sun was shining straight into her face, highlighting every little line. Obediently, Bianca lifted the cup to her lips and took a sip.

"I'm sorry you had to go through that," said Madame after a lengthy pause. "And on your very first day at my school."

Bianca was about to respond but the headmistress continued. "Well, at least I can offer you the best support that we have available. Here at the Europa International School we are fortunate to have close connections with the university. You know, of course, that our optional courses are given in part by associate professors from the university. One of them is a very good psychologist, Dr. Hasenberg, and he's here at the school at least once a week. So if you'd like..."

"No, thanks," said Bianca. "It's nice of you to offer, but I can deal with what happened last night on my own. I'm just overtired." Was she coming across as an emotional wreck?

Madame Lalonde frowned. Bianca had the feeling that she was analyzing her words, holding them up to the light and moving them back and forth, like a doctor looking at an X-ray. She made an effort to return the headmistress's gaze nonchalantly. Madame's eyes were a clear light green—but an unusual dark outside ring sharply contrasted with the iris. It was a mesmerizing, frighteningly intense gaze.

"I'll understand if you want to return home for a while after this shock," the headmistress said finally. Her voice sounded warm and caring. "If you want, you can come back in a couple of weeks." The cup felt like a lead weight in Bianca's hands. Her home flashed before her eyes: her father bent over a radio he'd taken apart, his brow deeply furrowed; her mother coming home from work, pale, but her step energetic, on her feet the scuffed, sensible shoes that she wore late into the night in the corridors and restaurant of the Mountain View Hotel. The image seemed foreign to her now, and it did not feel like home. She remembered Joaquim's words: "...not good enough for this school." Statements like that shouldn't bother her, not her, the

Bianca who made a point to *never* cry. Nevertheless, tears suddenly filled her eyes. She fumbled around in her jeans pockets until she unearthed a crumpled tissue. From the corner of her eye she saw that Madame Lalonde was standing up, and the next moment she felt a hand on her shoulder.

"If you don't feel up to studying after this incident, we could delay your application for six months. You wouldn't even need to reapply—your scholarship would simply be postponed until..."

"No!" The word slipped out more violently than she had intended. She would hold on to this opportunity the school was giving her. To Bianca's surprise, the headmistress laughed.

"Don't break the poor cup! No one wants to send you away from here, least of all me. I'm happy to be able to admit such a good student. I have read your application carefully—you're interested in taking psychology at university?"

Bianca nodded.

"Well, I think you have what it takes. Your determination to stay here, for one, shows me that you're not easily held back." Madame Lalonde smiled and suddenly seemed very likable. Her honey-colored hair shone in the morning sun. "You know, I was certain you'd stay. I'm not often wrong in my assessment of new students." With these words, she went back to her desk. Bianca heard the scraping sound of a drawer being opened. Madame Lalonde continued speaking as she pulled out several pieces of paper. "You're very bright, that's clear. But you sometimes have a sharp tongue, am I right? I think that on the inside you're quite different." Her eyes were soft and kind. "I was very similar as a young girl. I'm sure you'll fit in very well here."

"Well, that's not what the Wolves think." The words just slipped out. "Is it true that one night they threw a student into the river?"

Madame Lalonde's eyes turned serious again.

"Who told you that?"

"A new student—he heard it on his way here."

Madame Lalonde sighed and pushed a loose strand of hair behind her ear.

"Yes, that story's been going around for quite a while—it's as persistent as an urban legend," she said. "In all the time that I've been the headmistress here, though, I've never received a complaint like that. What's more, I can hardly imagine how anyone supposedly kidnapped a student from his room and transported him to the river without being noticed." She sighed. "And with regard to the Wolves... well, I can't say that I approve of everything they do. They have their own special rites, their code of behavior, and their... tests of courage, just like any other student association. They belong to the school as much as the exhibits in the museum and the old chestnut trees in the park. They've been a tradition here for over fifty years." She smiled again. "So far, every student has found his place here—as long as they arrive with the necessary staying power. But I'm not worried about that in your case. If you should have any problems with the Wolves, you can always come to me for help."

Wonderful, thought Bianca. Now I'm a tattletale!

"Another thing I should tell you," Madame Lalonde continued, "is that I've decided to put you in with the students in the senior class, rather than with the new students. Caitlin O'Connell will help you settle in. She comes from Ireland and will soon be taking her final exams. She'll be in the adjoining room in your dorm."

"I don't need any help," Bianca protested. "I'm not sick—I just stumbled across a dead body last night. I'll get over it."

"Of course. But I'm sure that you'll like Caitlin. Math is one of her strongest subjects."

Bianca looked up in interest. Well, that was different. She drank the last of her tea and nodded. "Agreed," she said, trying to smile. "For now, at least. But… there's something else..." She swallowed hard and asked the question that Detective Sinclair had not wanted to answer for her. "The dead woman…" She saw the headmistress stiffen slightly. "She broke her neck when she fell, didn't she?"

Madame Lalonde rested her elbows on her desk. "As far as we know at present, yes, it looks like it," she said finally.

"Detective Sinclair is from the homicide squad?"

"Yes. In the case of a sudden death like this, the first thing they do is check to see if it could have been murder. Especially since we have no idea at all who the woman was or how she got into the building."

"The door was open."

"I know. You told Detective Sinclair. Well, she wouldn't be the first one to break in."

"What could she have been looking for?"

"Do you any idea how much one page of our seventeenth-century convent chronicle is worth?" She seemed to be struggling to regain her composure. "However, it's not our problem. It's the job of the police, and the police alone, to figure out what happened." With these words the headmistress shut her desk drawer firmly. There was a knock at the door that made Bianca jump.

"Come in," called Madame Lalonde, her matter-of-fact headmistress's voice returning. A stocky, broad-shouldered man entered. When he realized that Madame Lalonde was not alone, his eyebrows arched. Bianca had seen him before. He was the janitor, she remembered. A crabby old fellow who looked like he had drunk too much for the last thirty years. The fine veins on his nose shone red and dark purple. Even so, his sports jacket looked custom-made. Bianca had never seen a janitor wearing a sports jacket before. But then, did anything at all at this school seem normal?

"The chairs and lamps are here," he growled. "You have to sign the delivery slip. And the electrician wants to know where you want him to put the lamps."

"Of course," agreed Madame Lalonde. "Bianca, please excuse me for a few minutes."

Her step brisk, the headmistress exited the office. Bianca heard the bunch of keys the janitor had fastened to his belt jangling with every step. With no eyes on her at last, the tension began to melt away. Wondering how long Madame might be, she drew back her arm, aimed, and threw the crumpled tissue in the direction of the waste bin beside the desk. It hit the edge of the bin, fell on the floor, and rolled away, toward the chair behind the desk.

Bianca got up and wandered over to the desk. She glanced out of the corner of her eye toward the half-open door, but to her relief saw nothing and heard no steps. So she ducked behind the desk, grabbed the tissue, and stood up again. So this was what the world looked like from Madame Lalonde's perspective. From here she could see not only the whole office, but also part of the hallway and—through the window—the main entrance and the park. If she had been sitting at her desk last night, she would have seen the Wolves setting out to fetch the new students. Much more interesting to Bianca than the view, however, was the stack of papers on Madame Lalonde's desk. Bianca noticed a drawing that looked like a branching geometric diagram. Only when she stepped closer did she realize it was some sort of family tree. She set down her empty cup and leaned in to get a better look. Instead of names, abbreviations were entered, as well as symbols that looked very scientific. The principles of association were easy to recognize: connections were shown by two interlocking rings. To Bianca, it looked like the intersection of mathematical sets. Each intersection formed a child—and in one place, even two children. "Dr. Florian Hasenberg" was noted in shorthand at the bottom of the page.

Bianca heard the sound of jangling keys approaching. She jumped, and stumbled over something soft and shapeless. She caught herself before she fell, grabbing the edge of the desk for support. She shook off the object that had caught her foot. It was a light-colored leather bag. She bent down quickly and pushed it back to where it had been leaning against the desk. The leather was as soft as a suede jacket and in good condition, though clearly not new. Something on the flap caught Bianca's eye—interlacing initials burned into the leather: an "M" and a "J."

The next moment Bianca was sitting in her chair again, her heart beating wildly. The headmistress and the janitor entered the room a second later.

"Mr. Nemec will take you to your dorm now. Bianca will be rooming with Caitlin O'Connell for the time being."

The janitor studied Bianca and then nodded. His glance traveled to the desk, as if drawn by a magnet. Bianca blushed furiously. There was her cup, right beside Madame Lalonde's papers.

The telephone rang.

“Lalonde,” the headmistress answered. Her expression was matter-of-fact, but then her glance fell on Bianca, and her voice became friendlier. “Of course. Just a moment, please.” She smiled encouragingly at Bianca. “It’s your father. He says he can’t reach you on your cell.”

Bianca jumped up and shook her head. “Tell him I’m fine and I’ll call him. Please!” For a few long seconds she looked imploringly into Madame Lalonde’s strange eyes. There was an unfamiliar but not unpleasant feeling of closeness. Madame Lalonde hesitated briefly, then glanced at the janitor, nodded and took her hand off the mouthpiece.

“Come with me,” grunted Mr. Nemec. He turned around and jangled out of the room.

CAITLIN

CAITLIN CAME FROM the Irish coast, near the town of Dingle. She did not fit the stereotype of the redheaded Irish girl, but had short brown curls that danced in all directions. She did have green eyes, though, and they shone like light-colored malachite. The introductions were friendly, but a little cool. But after Mr. Nemec left, and they had exchanged their first words, Caitlin seemed relieved and gave Bianca a genuine smile.

"Welcome to your new kingdom." Caitlin motioned toward a narrow bed, a desk, and a dresser. Not exactly elegant, but not uncomfortable either. Through the narrow window Bianca could see the visitors' parking lot, and she glanced at the hill behind it, where the orphans' cemetery was located. A shiver ran up her spine.

"The rooms in this building were originally a lot bigger, but since we keep getting more and more students, they had to renovate this old teaching wing," said Caitlin. "The rooms were divided in two—and most have this adjoining door. Some of the students move their dresser to block the door, but Jenna—the girl who moved out of here three weeks ago—and I usually just left it open during the day."

Indeed, in the middle of the wall to the left was a simple wooden door. Bianca finally put down her heavy knapsack and suitcase and followed Caitlin into the next room. It was like entering another world. A colorful patchwork quilt covered the bed, with a well-worn plush crocodile stretched out on it. Around the window was a string of red heart-shaped lights, and the whole wall was covered in photos, cards, and mementos, all pinned to the wallpaper with thumbtacks. One was of Caitlin with two boys who had the same green eyes as she did. They had their arms around each other and were laughing into the camera. "My brothers, Aidan and Paul," said Caitlin with obvious pride. "And in this picture here, that's my little sister, Kathy. That's my Mum and that's my Da, and that's my friend Deirdre. When I've finished here, I'm going to Trinity College in Dublin. Deirdre's going to apply, too. Maybe we'll even be able to get jobs as teachers at the same school." Her words echoed in Bianca's head. Caitlin's room intimidated her—so warm, cozy, and safe. There were presents from her family everywhere. You'd never know that her door led out to a hallway lit by fluorescent lights and not the living room of her parents' house in Dingle. "Don't you have any photos of your family?" asked Caitlin, when a little later Bianca pinned a poster of the solar system onto her wall.

"No," said Bianca, a little too abruptly.

"Or of your boyfriend?" Caitlin eyes twinkled. "You must have one!"

Bianca pressed her lips together and shook her head. That was all she needed—her roommate reminding her about Alex.

"Sorry. Did I say something wrong?" Caitlin wasn't giving up. "Did you two break up?"

"What else do you want to know?" Bianca snapped. "My shoe size?"

It was supposed to sound like a joke. Caitlin looked at her thoughtfully but didn't ask any more questions. Bianca choked back her tears, unpacked her things, and began her new life.

IT WAS NOT QUITE AS EASY as she had thought it would be. As soon as she closed her eyes, she saw the woman in the rumpled coat. That first night in her new much-too-soft bed, several times Bianca caught herself running her fingers over her neck, lost in thought. How bad did a fall have to be, to break your neck? Even after all the noises from the neighboring rooms and hallways had died down, the formulas, numbers, and calculations that normally sent Bianca off to sleep weren't working. Counting did not help, either, nor did visualizing imaginary numbers, which flared up briefly in the darkest corners of her imagination and then faded away again. Not even the thought of her problems with her parents could distract her from the woman with the gray curls. Her face kept coming back to her, her lips moving as she tried to tell Bianca something. Bianca went over every detail of this stranger's face in her mind, someone she had only seen for a few moments. It seemed important to picture her alive. She had a dimple in one cheek—it must have looked nice when she smiled. But her forehead was furrowed with worry lines. What had brought her to the school library? Bianca couldn't shake the memory of that hand poking out from its sleeve—the hand of a grown woman, with fingernails chewed down to the quick, like those of a nervous thirteen-year-old.

DESPITE THE INVESTIGATION, the new semester at the Europa International School began as planned. Only the library was closed. Every time Bianca looked out her window into the parking lot, a police car was there. And for the first few days, Bianca was a novelty for her fellow students. More than once she noticed students poking one another and nodding toward her. But she didn't have much time to feel annoyed.

Her course load was very heavy. At times Bianca envied Caitlin for having already made it through most of her studies, with just the final exams to go. The hours in class seemed to fly past, but the mountain of books that she apparently had to master before those first few preliminary exams in a few weeks did not get any smaller.

Although there were a number of mandatory subjects that scarcely interested Bianca, the course in probability theory was a revelation. The professor, Dr. Kalaman, gave the impression of being strict and brilliant, and every sentence he uttered was absolutely clear. Bianca followed him readily along the paths of histograms, frequency polygons, and distribution function, though she stumbled on some of the newer concepts and spent many hours at her desk after class happily trying to catch up. For the first time in several weeks, she had the feeling that she could at least grab at the fluttering, flyaway fabric of her life and hold on to it, at least by one corner...

Caitlin was amazed to learn that when Bianca was studying, she was completely oblivious to the ringing of the phone in the hallway—a piercing noise that the residents of the student quarters, many of them plagued by homesickness, could hear through the walls even in their sleep. Bianca's father managed to reach her once, but the conversation was stilted and carefully friendly, which ruined Bianca's mood for a whole day.

Whenever she was outside, Bianca would surreptitiously look over at the groups of older students who liked to hang out at the entrance to the cafeteria, but for the first few days she did not see Joaquim or any of the other Wolves. At the end of the week, however, she noticed Mr. Nemec entering the cafeteria with a tall stack of papers. A girl from Caitlin's volleyball team walked toward Bianca with her thumb pointed back over her shoulder.

"Did you hear?" she asked casually. "They've figured out how the woman died."

Bianca set off at a run. From some distance away she could see the students crowding around the bulletin board in front of the cafeteria. A girl protested as Bianca wedged herself in beside her. She felt elbows in her ribs, but finally she was at the front of the crowd and could read the photocopied newspaper article. "... The dead woman was identified as 54-year-old Annette Durlain from Brest, in Brittany," a student standing beside Bianca read aloud. "Her passport and luggage were found in a locker at the railway station. On the afternoon of her death, the woman had visited the Convent Museum at the Europa International School with a group of tourists." In several places Detective Sinclair was quoted. "Why the woman was in the Europa International School at night has not yet been determined." Her death, the article continued, had definitely been caused by a fall down the stairs. The investigation had concluded that no one else was involved.

"So it was an accident, after all," said a boy squeezed in next to Bianca. Bewildered, Bianca let herself be pushed back until she was again standing apart from the group. An accident. The word sounded all wrong, as if someone had said "afternoon nap" but really meant "coma."

Bianca buried her hands in her pockets and began to walk away. Beside the entrance hung a sign announcing the new schedule for tours of the Convent Museum. In this school they really did not waste much time on dead strangers.

"Hey, Bianca!" Although she had run a fair way to catch up to Bianca, Caitlin was not out of breath. Her curls were still wet from the shower. "I just heard." She grinned and pushed her hair off her face. Her roommate still bore the scent of workout clothes and the rubber of the worn basketballs from the gym. "That means they'll open the library again, early next week at the latest," Caitlin continued. "Thank heavens. I was starting to think I'd have to study shut up in my little room right up until the exams."

Bianca stopped abruptly. "Is that all you lot care about?" she snapped.

"What's the matter?"

"It's a miracle that anyone has even noticed that she was a person, not just 'the dead body,' or the reason you can't go into the library."

Caitlin looked at Bianca in astonishment and then held up her hands. "Sorry—I didn't realize you were taking it so much to heart. What on earth do you expect us to do? Hold a funeral service for her?"

"That would be better than nothing."

Caitlin pulled a face and shook her head. For the first time, Bianca saw anger flash in those green eyes. "Bianca, you know I'm not a monster. But... well, the woman was here and had an accident. That's tragic, and terribly sad. But... life goes on for us—school is hard, the demands they make on us are even harder, and when you've taken your first exam you'll see that we can't afford to waste even a single day. That's just the way it is. I'd like it to be a bit less stressful, but it's not."

Bianca stared at the ground. She really wanted to snap at Caitlin, to tell her to spare her the lecture, but she took deep breaths and restrained herself.

"I'm not stupid," she said quietly. "Believe it or not, I've already noticed that classes are still being held. But I simply can't believe... she was in the museum in the afternoon—but she died after midnight. What was she doing in between?"

"Presumably chasing ghosts," came the dry reply.

"What?"

Caitlin spread her arms. "Maddalina of Trenta," she said melodramatically. "Her witch's robe is hanging in the museum."

"And?"

"She haunts this place. I don't want to give you nightmares, but there have been students and teachers who have sworn that someone was following them. Some even claim to have heard the poor little orphan children crying. Then there's the groaning, scraping, howling—the whole deal."

Caitlin rolled her eyes and continued, "If you only knew how often someone or other who's into witchcraft stands in front of that glass case as if it were a shrine. Once a woman from a society that called itself the "New Witches" tried to hide in the museum so that she could spend a night beside Maddalina's robe. Crazy, huh?" She laughed. "Man, they should come to Ireland some time and stay in some of our castle ruins."

"The woman was going to hide in the library until dark and then go down to be near the witch's robe in the basement?"

"She was just unlucky enough to learn the hard way that the stairs aren't lit up at night."

"I'll say. Isn't the museum locked up?"

"Yes, of course. But other people have broken in, or tried to pick the lock." Bianca fell silent. The dead woman had not had any tools with her, unless she had hidden them under her coat. Bianca let her gaze wander back to the notice with the opening times of the museum. *Let it go!* whispered a very sensible voice in her head. *Just do your homework; the rest is none of your business.* Bianca listened to this voice for two or three heartbeats, then came to a decision. *So, this place is haunted,* she thought. *And Annette Durlain simply fell down the stairs?*

STICK DANCE

ON SATURDAY MORNING, Bianca woke from a strange dream in which Annette Durlain came to her and tried desperately to tell her something. Because it was the weekend, the school building was deserted, but outside there were people everywhere. A constant stream of cars turned into the visitors' parking lot; parents and brothers and sisters arriving for a weekend visit. Bianca felt a stab of sadness when she saw a girl running up to her father and hugging him. She looked at her watch. Four more hours until the tour of the Convent Museum. In front of the manor house, where the boys had their rooms, the first tourists were already being led through the buildings. One group was admiring the columns on either side of the doorway, which gave the building a temple-like appearance. Fingers pointed up at the stone statues, imposing women who gazed down at the people below with solemn faces. Bianca hitched up her knapsack full of books and set out for the park bench by the chestnut grove. Caitlin had been right about one thing: nobody here could afford to waste even a single hour. Bianca would have to write the first preliminary exam in two weeks. The books weighed heavily on her shoulders as she passed the open sports fields. The May sun had long since burned off the morning mist. The orange all-weather tracks glistened, and the area that served as both soccer pitch and athletics field was deserted. Bianca picked up the pace, walking briskly along the hedge that marked the front edge of the sports fields. A *thwack,* sharp as the crack of a whip, interrupted her thoughts. The sound came from the right—from behind the hedge she heard another *thwack.* A throaty, long drawn-out cry pierced the air. Bianca tightened her grip on her knapsack. She hesitated before cautiously approaching the hedge. Slowly she stretched out her hand and pushed a few of the branches aside. Part of the lawn came into view, and a spiraling piece of fabric. She leaned further forward and looked through the gap, almost losing her balance. Terrified, she recoiled. A branch snapped back over her fingers. Suddenly it all came back: the night in the park, the stick whistling past her face, the fear—and the dead woman. Bianca took a deep breath and wiped the beads of sweat from her forehead. Coward! she scolded herself. And yet—curiosity won over fear. Her heart pounding, she stepped closer to the hedge again.

Without the masks and furs, the Wolves did not look nearly so threatening. Joaquim was practicing doggedly. He landed every blow perfectly. Reluctantly, Bianca had to admit that she admired his coordination and quick movements. His partner, a girl with short, dark-brown hair, dodged Joaquim's swing deftly, springing aside. Two other Wolves joined the circle and hemmed in Joaquim—as if to capture him. It seemed to be the enactment of an ancient, ritualistic story. With narrowed eyes, Bianca observed the two newest fighters—a wiry boy, with light-brown hair bleached by the sun and a pale boy with his hair tied back in a ponytail. Was he the one who had worn the iron mask?

A fifth fighter, one Bianca hadn't noticed at first, was a girl with freckles. Her movements seemed rather playful and dance-like. She avoided the thrust of Joaquim's stick, twisting away. Her copper hair streamed behind her; she twirled around—and hit Joaquim in the shoulder. Bianca heard a dull thud and winced involuntarily. The blow had landed! Joaquim bent over in obvious pain. Stunned, he stared at the stick dancer. In an instant his face reddened with anger. The girl returned his gaze and stood still. The other Wolves seemed to have been turned to stone. Bianca held her breath. The game was over. The wind blew away Joaquim's words, but Bianca could follow what was happening, just from watching him slowly straighten up.

The red-haired girl grasped her stick firmly. She took a step backwards and slammed her weapon onto the ground. She shouted a retort, but all Bianca caught were the last few words: "... along with it any more!" Bianca pushed further into the shadow of the hedge, until her shoulder was brushing against the wall of green. Leaf tips tickled her cheek.

The dark-haired girl stepped forward and whispered something to the redhead. The other two Wolves just stood there, uncertain what to do. The redhead shook her head violently. The other girl tried to touch her arm—a soothing, conciliatory gesture, but she snapped at her and shook off her hand. Strangely, all the noises around them seemed to have disappeared. Bianca could no longer hear any laughter, any twittering of birds, not even the rustling of the chestnut trees.

The redhead left. Joaquim turned, his shoulders drooping, and watched her go. Through the gaps in the hedge, his face was framed with green leaves. It bore an expression that Bianca would never have expected. He looked frightened.

The Wolves' eyes met in silent agreement. Bianca swallowed. She would have liked to have jumped out from the hedge and warned the girl to run, but it was too late.

They shot into action simultaneously—four against one. The redhead skillfully parried a few strokes, but then she screamed and went down, gasping. Her freckled face distorted with pain. Bianca could see a bright red mark on her right upper arm.

The Wolves stood before her in battle formation. Bianca was afraid they would attack her again, but they suddenly let their weapons drop. Joaquim licked his lips, concentrating. The redhead gazed up into their dark faces, at a loss as to what to do. She grimaced, then howled with rage. Finally she stood up, retrieved her stick, and turned away.

RUNNING WITH THE HEAVY KNAPSACK wasn't easy. Bianca was panting by the time the parking lot finally came into view again. Her desire to study had completely left her. To avoid the sports fields, she had taken the long way back, going all the way around the manor house. The last thing she needed was to be discovered by the Wolves. She spotted a couple of tourists and felt a little better. She would feel even safer when she was back in her room, and looked up to her window in anticipation. The day seemed colder all of a sudden. The sudden crunch of gravel startled Bianca, but she suppressed the impulse to run. Certain it was Joaquim behind her, with his fighting stick at the ready, she turned around.

The redhead was clearly as surprised as Bianca. She jerked to a halt. Her sports bag hung from her left shoulder—and she was also carrying three practice sticks, each one a different length, under her left arm. Bianca noticed the welts on her right arm, already turning blue. Now the girl raised her injured arm and wiped her mouth and nose with the back of her hand. Her eyes were puffy, as if she had been crying all the way from the sports fields.

"What are you doing here?" she asked quietly.

"Studying," Bianca answered promptly. "And you? What did you have to do to make the others let you go?"

She indicated the welts and the girl flinched, as if she had just received another blow on the same spot. "I saw what happened," Bianca said softly. "They're pressuring you. Because you don't want to keep doing something with them, right?" The girl cast a venomous look in her direction.

"So, now you're meddling in our affairs?"

"Interesting that after that beating you're still talking about 'your affairs.' What was it you didn't want to go on doing?"

"That's none of your business."

"Does it have anything to do... with me?"

Without warning, the girl's arm flashed up. Before Bianca could figure out what was happening, a stick was flying toward her. Instinctively, she reached for it. Her palms hurt from the impact, but she held the stick firmly in her grasp. Her mouth went dry with shock.

"Good reaction," remarked the girl, putting down her bag. Bianca could see an airline tag and read the name on it: Sylvie Kay.

"What was that for?" she asked.

"The stick's heavier than it looks, isn't it?" This was true—and Bianca realized how powerful Sylvie's delicate-looking hands must be, to swing the long stick so quickly.

In one smooth move, the girl laid the two other sticks down on the ground, picked up the shorter one with her left hand, and swung it once in a graceful circle over her head.

"It won't help to run and hide," she said seriously. "If you want to stay at this school, you'll have no other option but to fight."

"Against you lot? Why should I? I have nothing to do with you."

Sylvie laughed bitterly.

"Nothing at all," she said, and pulled her arm back, ready to take a swing. Bianca recognized that it was a slowly executed practice move. It gave her enough time to grip the stick in her hand more firmly and parry the attack. Sylvie's stick cracked against the wood of her own, and Bianca could feel the jarring in every joint of her fingers. She stepped back and let her stick drop.

"I don't want to," she said firmly. "I'm here to study."

Sylvie curled her lip scornfully and leaned on her weapon.

Bianca decided to meddle some more. "You should report it to Madame Lalonde," she said. "I don't know what it is you don't want to do, but they have no right to beat you up. If you want, I can tell her what I saw."

"Madame? Phew, now I feel so much better," answered Sylvie, her voice dripping with sarcasm. "Make no mistake about it. She can't stand losers. She's very nice, sure, but try going to her and showing her you're a problem case or a coward. There's no room for those at an elite school. Have you ever wondered why two-thirds of the students don't pass the preliminary exams?"

Bianca gripped her stick harder. Two-thirds?

Sylvie gave a little laugh when she saw her face. When she continued, her voice sounded hard. "Just so we're clear here: no one 'beat me up.' When you practice, you get bruises. Understand?"

Almost before she was aware that Sylvie had moved, Bianca noticed a sharp pain in her lower arm.

"Are you crazy?" cried Bianca. It had not been a strong blow, but her skin was smarting all the same. Before even being conscious of what she was doing, she had snatched up her stick and attacked. Sylvie parried the blow with an expert, almost lazy, movement. Bianca had trouble reacting, the stick whistling through the air so quickly. There was a *thwack*. The crossed sticks hung in the air.

"That's better," said Sylvie. "You have good reactions. When I can only use my left hand, like now, you could even make things difficult for me."

Bianca lowered her stick and dropped it at Sylvie's feet. "It's not my thing," she replied. "You're really all crazy."

"Your decision. But in that case, be sure to lock your door." Sylvie laughed. "In fact, you'd best lock all the doors you can find."

"Oh, I assume that Joaquim will break the door down if he needs to." Bianca did not quite manage the scornful tone she'd been aiming for.

"Who's talking about Joaquim?" asked Sylvie quietly. She gave Bianca one last superior smile and picked up the sticks. "Have fun on the tour," she said, leaving a dumbfounded Bianca standing in the parking lot.

ABOUT TWENTY TOURISTS crowded around the door of the Convent Museum. Most of them were leafing through the brochure, not much different from the one included in the information folder for new students. Here too there was a diagram of the foundation of the old convent, and an aerial photo of the orphans' cemetery. Realizing that the dead woman had also waited at this door, Bianca felt like a thief slinking into a forbidden room. Gingerly she ran her fingers over the red mark on her lower arm—soon it would turn into a bruise. The Wolves were planning something, of that she was sure. The society was not as innocent as Madame believed. And how had Sylvie known that Bianca wanted to take the tour? Caitlin was the only one she had told about it. Would Caitlin...? Bianca shivered and pulled her jacket sleeve down to cover the red mark. Beside her, two tourists were talking quietly in rapid French. A huge camera lens dangling from the man's neck was aimed directly at Bianca. Seldom had she felt so exposed. When a rhythmic jingling approached, all conversation died. Bianca moved inconspicuously behind the French couple.

Simon Nemec came around the corner and looked over the group of tourists. He recognized Bianca immediately and raised his eyebrows. In the fluorescent light of the hallway, the old man seemed like a ghost: his cheeks sunken with uneven stubble where his razor had missed. Silently, he moved past the group and opened the door.

The room they entered in single file had a low ceiling, and the walls were paneled in light, sweet-smelling wood. The parquet flooring was so old that in some places it had bowed under the weight of countless footsteps. The colors of the various types of wood used for the parquet made a pattern of curved geometric figures in which Bianca could not help immediately seeing intersections and ellipses. Columns divided the room into a small main area and a walkway surrounding it—the architecture was probably supposed to be reminiscent of a convent's cloister. The tourists fell silent and looked around, awestruck.

Along the walls stood rows of glass cases containing exhibits. On the wall opposite the entrance hung the impressive fragment of an old door, the original entrance to the convent, decorated with an intricate carved relief. Of the twelve apostles who had once looked out at every visitor, only six remained—the left side of the door was missing.

Nemec was not a gifted tour guide. In a monotonous voice he reeled off the information. "In 1641, Maddalina of Trenta took over the leadership of the Belverina convent. Most of the documents from this time were destroyed after the witch trial and the dissolution of the order and its orphanage that followed it. The only thing that remains is a part of the original transcript of the trial of the Abbess. In addition, the Maddalina von Trenta Foundation managed to buy back some of the art treasures that once were used in the convent from private owners. Like this monstrance, for example."

He indicated a display cabinet. In it stood a vessel decorated with a burst of golden rays. The French couple leafed through a tiny dictionary. A younger couple were whispering together and smirking about Nemec's slurred pronunciation. Bianca looked at the janitor and realized that he had probably been drinking.

"And here you see the witch's robe," he continued. "Maddalina of Trenta wore it during the interrogations." With these words he turned a switch on the wall. The effect was well calculated—a murmur ran through the group. Bianca shuddered. In the display case a worn, coarsely woven robe was illuminated. Almost invisible nylon threads held it suspended. In the places where the dress had rested on collar bones and breasts, metal coat hangers shone through the threadbare fabric and somewhat suggested a body shape. It looked as if an invisible woman was wearing the long robe. Where the feet would have been there was paper covered with cramped writing—the transcript of the interrogation, as Mr. Nemec explained. Another light went on, illuminating an iron mask with horns and iron slits instead of eyes. It bore a remote resemblance to the mask that one of the Wolves had been wearing that night. "Note the needle near the mask of shame," continued the janitor. "It was used to test witches' marks. If an accused prisoner had an obvious birthmark or mole, their accusers stuck the needle into it. If the accused felt no pain and did not bleed, then it was declared a witch's mark." Nemec smiled coolly at the Frenchwoman, who was staring at him open-mouthed. "This original needle here, by the way, is a mechanical masterpiece and was clearly intended to deceive. When you press on it, it retracts into its shaft—no pain, no blood."

Bianca tried again to imagine the dead woman standing on this same spot. Had she read these words? And, if so, what had they meant to her? Bianca wondered if she, like Bianca, had looked at the transcript of the interrogation and tried to decipher the interlaced letters:

> *...He Ask'd Maddalina of Trenta [if she] Her Self had been Qveen of the Witches there [at the Witches Dances] amongst Witch People and Feends.*

Trying not to let Nemec see her, Bianca pulled out her notebook and copied the words down exactly as they were written. She looked several times to be sure that "Feends" really had two "e"s. Just as she was finishing, a tingling sensation on the back of her neck made her lift her eyes from her notebook and look around. At first she was scared, because she thought she saw the boy with the sun-bleached hair from the Wolves, but then she breathed a sigh of relief. It was only a tourist, one she had not noticed before. Tall and gaunt, this tourist had buried his hands in the pockets of his leather jacket. His blond hair shone in the light of the display case. He was looking at the vessel in the other case—but his interest seemed feigned.

Bianca quickly turned back to the witch's robe, but this time she did not look at the exhibits but rather at the reflection in the glass. She could make out the French couple behind her, who were staring over her shoulder—and to the left stood Leatherjacket. She guessed him to be about eighteen. He did not look like someone who would willingly spend his free time looking at historical exhibits. And she was right: as if he had been waiting for her to turn away, he turned his head to look at her again. In the reflection, she could make out his serious face and narrow, curved lips. With a strange intensity he studied Bianca from head to toe, as if memorizing what she looked like. She stepped to one side, avoiding his gaze. "Who's talking about Joaquim?" Sylvie's words rang in her head. Uneasy, she stared at the glass panes of the case, which had been sealed with silicone. Had Annette Durlain stood here too—observed by a stranger? Bianca noticed that in some places the silicone seemed new—transparent and untouched, like fresh ice cream. A tourist moved closer, jostling her a little. Gratefully, she crouched down, half hidden behind the glass, and examined the hem of the witch's robe. She noticed something right at the bottom. She frowned and leaned a little further forward. Near the frayed hem she could make out a dark spot. It must be a rust spot, but with a bit of imagination one could say it was blood.

DREAMS

THE SOUND OF THE KETTLE woke Bianca with a start. Her T-shirt was sticking to her body and she was trembling. The reading lamp, which she had turned on last night, was still on. The dream had been even worse than those of previous nights. The woman in the rumpled coat was trying to communicate with her again, but was prevented from doing so by Joaquim. He was roaring, lashing out with his fighting stick. For a moment Bianca thought she could still see the iron mask of shame that had whispered secrets into her ear; then this image disappeared too, leaving her alone in her damp, twisted sheets.

Her math book lay on the floor like a bird with its wings outstretched. She heard the birds in the orphans' park and slowly started to realize it was morning. She thought it odd that she couldn't detect any movement in Caitlin's room. Only the water bubbled, as if the kettle had been turned on by a ghostly hand. Usually Bianca could hear the patter of Caitlin's feet in the darkness and then the gurgling of water when she tipped the mineral water out of her bottle into the kettle—she never used tap water for her tea.

Bianca glanced over at the adjoining door, which was open just a crack. No movement. With a click, the switch on the kettle snapped to the "Off" position. The bubbling stopped. A moment later she heard the beeping of Caitlin's alarm, which she set on weekends too, so she wouldn't miss breakfast. Light showed through the gap in the door. Relieved, Bianca listened to her roommate's steps as she went over to the kettle. A second later she could hear Caitlin pouring water into cups. She rolled out of bed.

"Oh, good morning!" Caitlin always looked especially nice in the morning. Her cheeks were rosy and her tousled hair as yet untamed by gel. She opened her eyes wide in astonishment. "You look awful! Are you sick? Your eyes are all puffy."

Bianca forced a lopsided grin. "Headache," she said. "So now you have a remote control for the kettle?"

Caitlin reached for the wall plug and passed Bianca a bizarre-looking little box that attached to the plug. Bianca sat down on Caitlin's bed and turned it over in her hands.

"Radio-operated timer. Jan installed it yesterday while you were in the museum."

"Jan who?"

"You know who he is!"

"The guy in my year?"

Caitlin nodded. "He's nice," she said, with a knowing grin.

"Since when do you bother with children?"

"Children? Jan's nineteen!"

Bianca looked up from the timer switch, shocked.

"Really? He looks like he's fourteen! How many times did he have to repeat a year?"

Caitlin stopped laughing. "Ask him yourself! By the way, he

told me he thinks you're quite nice. I think he was disappointed that you weren't here yesterday."

"Really? Well, I think he's kinda weird—why would an artsy guy build switches like this?"

"Like I said—ask him yourself. It's OK to talk to people, Bianca!"

"Yes, you're a good example of that!" It slipped out a little too sharply and Bianca regretted her tone immediately.

"What's that supposed to mean?"

"Did you tell Sylvie that I was going on the museum tour?"

Now Caitlin was genuinely mystified.

"Was it a secret? No, I didn't tell Sylvie. But I might have mentioned to a few of the girls on my basketball team that you were going to go see Maddalina's robe. Why are you interrogating me?"

"I'm having really bad dreams."

"Don't change the subject—what's going on?"

Now Caitlin's voice sounded sharp. Bianca realized that she had gone too far. Resisting the urge to start screaming at her roommate, she pulled herself together. "Nothing," she muttered.

"Don't try to fool me! Since you went on that tour yesterday you've hardly said a word." Caitlin sat down on the edge of the bed and passed a cup of hot tea to her. "I'm serious, Bianca," she said more gently. "I'm not trying to tell you how to run your life, but you don't seem happy. Is there anything I can do?"

Bianca looked at her roommate thoughtfully. She really looked worried—and Bianca's mistrust suddenly seemed quite unfounded. Embarrassed, she pushed her hair back behind her ears and starting telling Caitlin what she had been waiting for.

"If I tell you—will you promise you won't try to persuade me to go to Madame Lalonde?"

"It's the Wolves, isn't it? Are you having problems with them?"

"They seem to be having a problem with me."

She told Caitlin about what she had seen at the sports fields and some of her conversation with Sylvie. She did not say anything, however, about Sylvie's warnings, her bruised arm, or the strange boy in the leather jacket.

"So that's it," said Caitlin, relieved. "Why didn't you tell me yesterday? You'd certainly have slept better last night. I already know about the argument. It was about the medieval festival. Every August, the city puts on a medieval market and the Wolves usually give a demonstration of stick fighting. Sylvie doesn't want to take part this time, so she backed out. Too much stress from schoolwork."

"And so they beat her up?"

"Listen, the Wolves have their own rules and they sort out their disagreements amongst themselves."

"Yes, that seems to be the way it is at this school. Everyone has to look after themselves."

"And only someone as prickly as you would say that," responded Caitlin with a smile. "You think everyone's out to get you. You don't notice that there are people here who like you, and you won't let them near you."

"And the rest of you seem to see nothing at all—a woman falls down the stairs and dies: so what? A student is hurt, just because she wants to back out of the medieval troupe: so? They have their own rules. Is there anyone here who cares about what happens to other people?"

To her surprise, Caitlin put her arm around Bianca's shoulders. "I care about what happens to you," she said. "It's just that this isn't like other schools. Here we all have to learn to solve our own problems. It's hard at the beginning, I know. But just to reassure you: yes, the Wolves are crazy. Some, by the way, are also quite nice. Tobias—the boy who goes around in the musician mask—went out for a while with Jenna, the girl who lived in your room."

"And?"

Caitlin laughed. "What do you want me to say? That he forced her to howl at the moon with him? All nonsense—the Wolves are simply a society, nothing more. Jenna and Tobias had an argument, and he broke up with her. But that certainly wasn't the Wolves' fault—more Tobias's, because he hung out too often with a girl from his chemistry class."

"And Joaquim?"

"Good athlete. Sometimes rather arrogant. And he has a short fuse—like yesterday. But it's not your job to protect Sylvie. We all have to make our own decisions."

"How many Wolves are there all together?" asked Bianca, after taking this all in.

"Joaquim, of course. Tanja, Tobias, Martin, and Sylvie. That's the core group."

"Is there... a blond boy in the group, one who wears a leather jacket?"

Caitlin frowned. "Hmm... not that I've noticed. Maybe among the newbies, but in any case they're mainly there for the stick training." Her smile widened. "Listen, I don't think the Wolves want anything from you. Even what they did on the first day—it was nothing personal. They always pick on one student to tease at the beginning. If I were you I wouldn't worry about it at all. Just hang in there for a couple more weeks. And if you're still being harassed, then come and tell me, OK? I promise I won't go running to Madame." She looked at Bianca directly. "And one day you'll have to tell me what your mother did that was so terrible that I always have to make excuses for you when she calls."

Bianca winced. "You think I've flipped for sure, don't you?"

Caitlin laughed and gave her a friendly push. "At first I was afraid you had," she admitted. "Madame's great, but because I'm the student president she makes me take on the problem cases. But anyone who's been through what you have would have bad dreams." Caitlin yawned and glanced at the clock radio. "C'mon! If we hurry, we'll still get breakfast." She jumped up and yanked open her dresser drawer, which squeaked in protest. Bianca took a sip of tea and stared into the amber liquid. It smelled of orange and vanilla.

THE LIBRARY WAS SUPPOSED TO REOPEN on Tuesday morning. Bianca was so impatient she could hardly focus on her class. As soon as the bell rang, she snatched up her things and was the first to leave the room. Today the hallways seemed particularly long. The other students made a beeline for the cafeteria, but Bianca turned down the hallway that led from the biology labs to the main entrance of the school. Above the high double door hung a plate of brushed steel, engraved with the school's motto: *Porta post portam*—an invitation to strive to open more doors of knowledge. Bianca stepped through the door into the open air. Suddenly she felt a hand on her shoulder. She turned around, terrified.

“Sorry,” panted Jan. “I didn’t want to frighten you—didn’t you hear me calling you?”

Bianca took a deep breath. “No. What’s up?”

He reached into his pocket and pulled out a crumpled piece of paper.

“From Mrs. Catalon. You left in such a rush that you didn’t hear her calling us back in. Worksheet—due the day after tomorrow.”

“OK. Thanks.”

Jan watched as Bianca folded the paper and absentmindedly pushed it into her bag.

“So?” he asked. “How are you?”

“Fine. Why?” Was this going to be a friendly chat, classmate to classmate?

“Caitlin said that you… were asking about me.”

All of a sudden Bianca caught on, and nearly groaned aloud. Two lonely souls who were destined to find each other. What a clever plan of Caitlin’s. Somewhere far down the hallway the last door clicked shut.

“Actually, I was just asking about that timer you built for the kettle.”

He was neither surprised nor disappointed. “It’s nothing special. I cobbled it together in class.”

“Are you taking a shop course, too?”

Jan grinned. He still looked fourteen, though he had a new haircut.

“No, only the art-project course. It’s called ‘Back to Metropolis.’ We’re building a model of this silent film town.”

All at once he became serious again and looked around anxiously. He stepped a little closer to her. Bianca noticed that he was no taller than she was. "Actually… I wanted to tell you that I'm sorry I abandoned you during the midnight tour. I really thought you were right behind me. If I'd known they were going to just leave you there, I would have gone back again."

"It's OK," Bianca replied. "Don't worry; it'll take a lot more than that to intimidate me."

Jan looked at her doubtfully. "I hope so," he said. "They don't seem to like you particularly."

"Well observed. Are you really nineteen?"

"Yes, that's right."

"Why are you only in the tenth grade?"

"Is this an interrogation?" he asked, annoyed. "I was out of school for a while."

"Were you… sick?"

"Yeah, something like that."

"And now you're interested in art."

"Actually just in clay." He grinned, leaned in closer, and whispered, "I didn't have such a great kiln at home."

He gave her a wink, turned on his heel, and headed down the empty hallway. Bianca's cell phone started to vibrate in her jacket pocket. She took it out and saw it was her mother. She sure didn't give up easily! Bianca stared at the display until the phone vibrated for the fifteenth time. Then she turned off the phone, jammed it back in her pocket, and wiped her eyes on her sleeve. The bruise on her arm hurt. Once again she felt that dull sense of emptiness.

THE LIBRARY WALLS WERE DARK from the powder the police had used to check for fingerprints. A note on the glass door warned that renovations were in progress. As Bianca entered the foyer with its reading tables, her stomach lurched and she felt like she was on a rollercoaster. Every trace of the dead woman had been eradicated. The stairs and the steel banisters had already been scrubbed clean, and the stone floor shone. Bianca stared at the spot where the woman had lain. Finally she plucked up her courage and, eyes lowered, slipped past, keeping as far away from the actual spot as she could.

The layout of the library was like the school: bathed in light, and its glass walls and brushed steel gave the rooms the appearance of a modern office building. The chairs were designed ergonomically and the reading lights looked like the outstretched arms of robots.

Feeling like an intruder, Bianca filled out her application for the language lab and got her user card for the computer workstations. She could feel her notebook with the notes she had made about Annette Durlain pressing against her. She stepped close to the glass facade that looked down onto the broad staircase and reading tables below. To the right of the drink machine a few students were using some of the small tables as a cafeteria. A blond boy wearing a leather jacket was not among them. She contemplated the spot at the foot of the stairs. For a moment, she imagined she could see the outline of a figure, and shuddered. How could Annette Durlain have fallen so awkwardly down those stairs? She had landed on the floor right beside the banisters—wouldn't she have automatically grabbed on to them to catch herself? Bianca looked around, and when she was sure no one was watching her, pulled out her notebook and sketched the stairs. She drew an outline of Annette Durlain's body, indicating its position as far as she could remember.

Behind her loomed seemingly endless aisles of steel shelves. Slowly Bianca turned around. "Languages," she read on a sign, and behind it "French III." A library full of school books. Annette Durlain had hidden here for seven hours. Bianca pushed her pencil back into her bag and began walking down the aisles, imagining Annette Durlain seeking out a spot to hide. It wouldn't have been easy. The shelves stood at right angles to the wall and you could see right through them. Even in the corner seating areas there was hardly anywhere you would be invisible. A narrow door led to a staircase, but it was locked. Not likely that Annette Durlain had had a key. Again and again Bianca took out her notebook and noted down the corners that offered some protection from view. On the far end, a wide door was ajar. Bianca ignored the "Private" sign and slipped in to the adjoining room. It smelled of old wood varnish.

It was another room full of books. Bianca walked up and down aisle upon aisle. Freud's works were here, and other psychology classics, such as the theories of C.G. Jung. Bianca noticed the worn carpet and stopped short. Some of the shelves were on casters—and one of them was slightly out of place. There was an obvious hollow where a caster had once pressed into the carpet. Quietly Bianca dropped to her knees and peered out over the spines of the books. Behind them there was only a wall—but was it possible to push the shelf aside and hide behind it?

She struggled to pull the shelf forward. She could only move it forward a centimeter at a time. The result was disappointing. The wall behind it was freshly painted. She could see a remnant of masking tape on a light switch. Obviously the shelf had only been moved because of the renovations. Bianca sat down on the floor and contemplated the lower rows of books of the adjacent shelf. "The Mechanisms of Selected Psychotropics" was the title on the spine of one of the thicker ones. Carefully she pulled the book out and began to leaf through it. Hundreds of technical terms. If you believed them, you could imagine man as a chemical construction kit. You just had to balance the substances, the hormones, the serotonin, the flow of adrenalin; everything followed a plan that could be figured out. Grief was quantifiable. Or was it?

She shut the book with a snap and looked up. She could hear something! She sat motionless and listened until she could make out the sound—sniffling. And it was coming straight from the next aisle. Bianca crawled closer to the bookshelf. Through the gap left by her book she could see dark jeans. Something jingled, a knee appeared, then the gap went dark—and suddenly she was staring into Simon Nemec's face.

"I thought it was you," he said in a husky voice. The strong peppermint smell of his breath did not quite cover the smell of alcohol. He disappeared and emerged again around the corner. The sports jacket that he always wore was worn at the elbows and looked shabby in the harsh noon light. Caught in the act, Bianca stood up.

"What are you up to?" he snarled.

Bianca gripped her notebook firmly and flashed an innocent smile.

"Research?" she said quietly. "Aren't we allowed to be in the library?"

Silently they regarded each other. Nemec's eyes were slightly red, as if he had a cold.

"There's no reason for you to be in here. This is part of the reference library, for the faculty only."

"Where does it say that?"

"In the library rules, which you have obviously not read. And what about the sign saying 'Private'? Did you read that?"

Bianca felt her confident smile melt away.

"I call this snooping," said Nemec. "And don't think I didn't notice that you were at Madame Lalonde's desk. Do we understand each other?"

Bianca's heart sank. The look she gave Nemec must have looked pathetic, for it elicited from him a grim smile. Hesitantly, Bianca nodded.

"Good." He leaned further forward and indicated the notebook that Bianca was still holding tightly. "And be grateful that I don't confiscate your notes," he said. "I bet I'd find a few things there that have nothing to do with your homework, eh?"

Only now did Bianca notice the fresh bandage on his right hand. "What did you do to your hand?" she asked quietly.

Nemec folded his arms and looked down at Bianca. "Slipped. Working on the renovations."

"Are you left-handed?"

"Why do you want to know?"

"Usually right-handed people are more likely to injure their left hand."

"I guess you think you're very clever," he said. "If you really want to be clever, then you'll return to the students' area, and quickly."

THE DREAMS STILL CAME like thieves in the night, creeping up to her bed and entering her head. Instead of the witch's robe, sometimes it was Bianca's mother in the display case now—a sad wax doll. She wore the red and white uniform of the Mountain View Hotel, which always made her look a bit too pale.

Annette Durlain, in her loose-fitting coat, was standing beside the display case. A face was reflected in the glass—Bianca had expected to see Nemec's features, but to her horror she realized it was the boy in the leather jacket. She did not dare to look to the left, straight into his eyes. Instead, she watched in the reflection as he reached inside his jacket and pulled out a gleaming witch's needle. It looked like a dagger. Bianca cried out and ran to the display case, but a wall of heat stopped her in her tracks. Her mother's features began to melt and dripped like skin-colored wax onto her uniform. Bianca called to her, but her voice sounded only like the creaking of a door. Suddenly a red-hot sun shone beside Bianca. It had a face and looked like an ancient copper engraving come to life. The rays flickered and only then did Bianca see the lion. The beast was gigantic, as big as the sun. Bianca stumbled backward and bumped into a hot wall. The lion crouched and sprang. Its claws drove into the sun, and it buried its fangs in the glowing sphere, biting into it as if into prey. The pungent smell of beast and soot was everywhere. The boy in the leather jacket raised the needle dagger. Annette Durlain doubled up in terror. The sun screamed.

Bianca woke up with a start and felt for the light switch with fingers slippery with sweat. Nothing happened. The room remained a black hole. Only the sound of the switch for her reading lamp, which Bianca kept flicking, disturbed the silence. Obviously the bulb had burned out. Bianca wiped her hands off on the sheet and stared into the darkness. She spent a while just trying to breathe calmly.

The silence in the dorm was oppressive. Bianca threw back the bedclothes and felt her way toward the door, her knees shaking. Luckily she had only pulled the blinds down halfway the night before. Gradually she could make out the outline of the chair, the door, and—beside it—the lighter patch of the overhead light switch. When it clicked she closed her eyes tightly, expecting a bright light. Nothing happened. A power cut—now, of all times! Uncertainly she reached out her hands again to feel her way back to her desk, hoping her keys were there. Yes. The keys clattered as she pulled them toward her and fumbled for the little LED flashlight attached to the chain. Through the wide gap between the blind and the window sill she could see a strip of the parking lot. She gave a start and stood still, not breathing, her keys in her hand. Someone was standing down there, half turned away from her. Bianca leaned forward over the desk. The jagged edges of the keys dug into her palm. She was dreaming. She must still be dreaming! Below the window stood Annette Durlain. The figure just stood there—black and shadowy, barely distinguishable from the night-gray gravel of the parking lot. Bianca squinted in an effort to make out the outline. The blurry shadow seemed to be changing shape. It could be a woman in a coat, yes—but suddenly the phantom almost looked like a man in a dark cloak. Nemec? she wondered. The Wolves? As if it had felt Bianca's gaze, the phantom jerked its dark head back and looked up, right at Bianca's window. At the same moment Bianca felt as if she had the vision of a cat. It seemed quite logical that she could now make out what it was wearing—a nun's habit? She felt rather than heard a voice reverberating deep within her, like an echo. There were no words, just a feeling, a certainty that something lay ahead for her—a battle, a... danger? A shadowy-black arm rose into the air, as if the phantom was waving to her.

Bianca darted to the side so quickly she banged her shin on the bed. The thing could not possibly have seen her in this dark room. Nevertheless her heart was beating wildly. She waited several minutes, which to her seemed like a whole day, and only then dared to take a careful look out the window—from the very edge, so she could pull back out of sight quickly. The figure had disappeared. Only a glimmer caught her eye. Perhaps it was a glass shard reflecting light from somewhere. And there was something that might have been a burning cigarette. Bianca sank onto her bed and pulled up the covers. Now she was sure someone was outside her door. Joaquim and the others—and Leatherjacket, who was waiting to drag her to the river. Maybe he was one of the Wolves. She got up and crept over to the door again. Once there, she laid her ear against the wood and listened. Of course she thought she heard a scraping noise. The door handle felt cool to the touch. Then it moved under her hand. Someone was pressing down the door handle! Bianca pulled her hand away as if she had burned herself. Breathlessly she watched the handle moving. Someone was checking whether the door was locked. The key chain fell out of her hand and landed on the carpet with a soft clink. At that moment the lights came back on. Startled, Bianca recoiled and crashed into the armchair near the door. It was many thousands of heartbeats later, it seemed, that she dared to reach out her hand for her umbrella, to use as a weapon if necessary. But the door handle was not moving any more. Quietly Bianca picked up the key ring and unlocked the door. Umbrella at the ready, she flung open the door. In the empty hallway the wall clock flashed 12:00. She grabbed her watch from the night stand: 3:48 a.m.

APOLLONIA

BIANCA HAD CONSTRUCTED a mountain of books at her spot at the reading table in the library. Yellow sticky notes stuck out from the pages. In two days she had to hand in her biology project, and tomorrow she would write the first preliminary exam, in history. History did not worry her, but now that her biology teacher, Mrs. Catalon, had left action potentials and nerves behind and moved on to genetics, Bianca felt as if two years of material had been squeezed into four weeks. She leaned back and peered through the aisles to the computer workstations. In twenty minutes the library computer that she had booked would be free. A girl with buck teeth was there now clicking through a data bank. Sighing, Bianca bent over her notes again and read through them for the hundredth time. She had to make it! There were no two ways about it—if she wanted to stay at the school, she had to pass the preliminary exams. But the words refused to find their way into her head; they slipped from her grasp and faded away. It was impossible to concentrate. Again and again she felt as if she were holding her door handle in her hand, and when she closed her eyes, the phantom waved to her.

Again she ran through all the possibilities she had thought of so far: it was Leatherjacket, and her eyes had played a trick on her in the dark. He had Annette Durlain on his conscience and in the Convent Museum had selected Bianca to be his next victim. Or was it Tanja, acting as lookout while the other Wolves tried to get Bianca out of her room and drag her to the river. Or—Maddalina of Trenta?

"Ridiculous!" whispered Bianca, putting her pencil down. She rubbed her eyes hard and red stars exploded behind her eyelids. Her thoughts ran in circles: Annette Durlain and Leatherjacket, Leatherjacket and the Wolves, the Wolves and Joaquim, Joaquim and Bianca… nothing made any sense. And yet she had the feeling that there *was* a connection. Exhausted, she pressed her palms to her eyes. She saw the gray-haired woman going down the stairs, step by step. Annette Durlain turned around and looked up at Bianca. In the shadows her face looked like a mask. She smiled, opened her arms wide—and fell backward. Bianca gave a start and blinked her eyes open. In the library all was silent. Exhausted, she stood up and went over to one of the wide, half-open windows. The fresh air felt good. From below she could hear the jubilant cry of a volleyball team, then a short blast from the referee's whistle. Bianca leaned her hot forehead against the windowpane and gazed at the path, and the hedge alongside it. She had to talk to Sylvie—as soon as possible.

A figure slowed its step and stopped on the path. Hastily Bianca pulled back and then carefully looked out of the window again. She needn't have bothered—the figure could not possibly recognize her from down there—the tinted glass facade acted like a mirror. The concentrated and furtive look with which Leatherjacket was surveying the building disturbed Bianca all the more. He had turned up his worn collar as if he were cold, and a cigarette drooped from the corner of his mouth. After a minute that seemed to last forever he went on his way and disappeared from view.

She only felt safe again when she was back at her reading desk, behind the stacks of books, which separated her from her surroundings like the walls of a fortress. She was about to pull the thick biology text towards her again when she stopped short. It was no longer open at the same place. Some passer-by must have caused a draft that had turned the pages. Then she looked at her other books. The sticky notes had disappeared, or had been set at different places in the books. An important reference work on genetics had disappeared. With a sudden sinking feeling in her belly, Bianca quickly lifted up the top page of her notes. Empty pages grinned mockingly up at her. She sprang up and looked around. Some students had left. Behind her, at the computer, stood the girl with buck teeth, packing up her things. Bianca sank down onto her chair and looked over her books again. One of them she had definitely not brought to the table. It was thick and slightly yellowed; its title indicated it contained legends of the saints. A paper protruded from between the pages, obviously marking a passage. She opened it. The passage described the martyrdom of Saint Apollonia. "All Apollonia's teeth were knocked out by her cruel torturers." Bianca swallowed hard and looked at the figure of the martyr, who was holding the symbols of her torture in her hand: forceps and a tooth. Someone had used a pencil to underline the words "knocked out." But what frightened her even more was the fact that they had also colored the saint's hair black, which made her look strangely like Bianca.

CAITLIN NEARLY DROPPED her water bottle with shock when Bianca rushed into the room. Bianca did not even seem surprised to see Jan sitting on the bed.

"What's wrong?" cried Caitlin, jumping up.

"My project's gone!" gasped Bianca. "Stolen!" Bianca spilled out the whole story. Jan listened for a while in silence, then stood up and went out without a word.

"Somebody's just playing a trick on you." Caitlin said soothingly.

"Bullshit! Someone's very serious about this. And this place marked in the book—that was a threat!"

"Bianca, calm down!"

"I don't know if it's Joaquim or not, but someone is trying to scare me off. Perhaps the guy in the leather jacket is part of it, too."

"What guy?"

"He's been watching me. He might even have been below my window one night recently."

"When?"

"The day before yesterday. There was a power cut," said Bianca. "And... there was somebody in the parking lot. In the middle of the night. He was staring up at our window."

Caitlin made a face, obviously skeptical.

"It's true!" persisted Bianca. "I didn't tell you, but he was standing down there as if he was looking for something."

The pause that followed grew uncomfortable, and Bianca already regretted telling Caitlin about it. Caitlin looked at her closely. Bianca could almost read her thoughts.

"I didn't dream it," she said with emphasis. "Someone was there."

"So what? Maybe he was at the club and was coming back late from town. Maybe it was the boyfriend of one of the girls in our building and he was throwing stones at her window."

"At four in the morning?"

Caitlin pressed her lips together.

"Think about it," she said finally. "Who was in the library? Joaquim?"

Bianca shook her head.

"Another of the Wolves?"

"No."

Caitlin was silent.

"You don't believe me, do you? You think I'm crazy."

Caitlin hesitated.

"Yes, of course I believe you," she said slowly. At that moment Jan came flying back into the room and threw an armful of papers and books onto the bed. Papers fanned out in all directions.

"This was at your seat."

Bewildered, Bianca stared at the papers. They were her notes.

"They were gone," she stammered. The look Caitlin and Jan exchanged spoke volumes.

"And where is the book about saints?" she asked, getting worked up. "I can prove it to you—someone drew a picture of me. That was a threat!"

"There was no book about saints there," said Jan calmly. "I even looked under the table."

"And the other books? Look—the sticky notes have all been moved around."

"Hmm," said Jan. "You come from a very respectable neighborhood, don't you? Where I come from people often give themselves an advantage by making life difficult for the competition. You're lucky your notes are still here."

"That makes no sense!" said Bianca.

"If you ask me, it does," replied Jan, "Don't leave your stuff lying around like that. Obviously you're not coping too well with the stress here."

Caitlin dug him in the ribs. Jan grinned apologetically and grabbed his jacket.

"OK, understood," he said. "See you!"

There was an uncomfortable pause while Jan's steps retreated down the hallway. Bianca took her notes and leafed through them page by page.

"There!" she cried. "Two pages are missing—and of course it had to be those with the classifications and the whole of the bibliography. Who would take the whole stack and then put everything back except for two pages?"

Caitlin stood up and smiled at her reassuringly. At this moment Bianca hated her "student-president" smile. "Have another look," said Caitlin. "Maybe you forgot to take those pages with you, or you've put them in the wrong place."

"Do I look as if I'm senile? I had them with me!"

"Do you know how you've seemed to me for the last couple of days? Like someone who's from another planet. Not only do you insist that we both lock our doors..."

"There's a reason for that!"

"What reason? Do you think someone's creeping around at night taking things? Geez, Bianca! Come back to earth!"

Caitlin folded her arms. Her smile had faded. Bianca sank onto her desk chair, snatched up her key chain, and looked for the drawer key. She tore the drawer open so roughly that all her notes slid forward, landing against the front edge of the drawer. Furiously, she took out the papers and binders and threw them onto the bed. Caitlin watched in silence as she searched through the pile.

"No notes," said Bianca finally. "I didn't leave the two pages here."

"I've had enough," said Caitlin. "If you really think the Wolves want to throw you into the river or scare you away, then we should go to Madame Lalonde right now."

"Definitely not," snapped Bianca, standing up. "Not a word to Madame! Or I might as well just go straight home! Promise, Cait?"

Her friend looked at her doubtfully, but finally she nodded. "Promise. Hey, where are you going?"

"To look for Sylvie."

"Sylvie? She won't be back for ten days."

"What? Why?"

"Her mother's sick. She went home," said Caitlin.

"Well, what a coincidence." The words had slipped out before Bianca could stop them.

Caitlin's green eyes flashed. She looked as if she wanted to shake Bianca to make her see sense. "She got permission and even registered her absence in the office. And this morning she took a taxi to the station. Doesn't quite have the appearance of a violent death, does it?"

"OK, OK," Bianca snapped at her, jumping up. "Don't worry —the lunatic with the persecution complex is now going peacefully to the library to fetch her jacket!"

Nothing had changed there. Once more Bianca went over every step in her head, trying to remember who had been in the room. Buckteeth was now sitting in the reading corner, busily making notes. A few other tables were empty, and Bianca wondered whether members of the Wolves might have been sitting there, and she had just not noticed them. Everything was the same as usual, except that she felt a threat lurking in every corner. With a shiver she left the room and went to the cloakroom. Just as she was reaching for her jacket, she noticed a figure standing behind the big glass wall on the second floor. Simon Nemec was standing right at the edge of the hall, between two shelves, where he could not be seen from the cafeteria. He just stood there, staring at the stairs. His face was red, and the corners of his mouth hung down like those of a sad clown. He raised his arm and wiped his eyes with his sleeve. It took Bianca several seconds to understand what she was seeing. The old janitor was crying.

LA BÊTE

THE HALLWAY IN FRONT of the offices was deserted. Nervously, Bianca stood in front of Madame Lalonde's door and waited. The message she had found stuck to her door after school was now limp and crumpled, she had handled it so much. The last time she was in this hallway, she had not noticed the big map of the world that filled up almost all the space between the two doors. It was dotted with innumerable tiny flags. Each blue flag represented a student, and each red flag, a teacher. The names were printed on them with black markers. Marie-Claire Lalonde came from Alsace and many students came from Austria, Holland, and Germany. Bianca's chemistry teacher came from London; other teachers came from France, Poland, and Slovakia. But there were also flags near Odessa and in Kiev. Bianca's gaze wandered toward Spain, to a little flag in Madrid. "Joaquim Almán," she read.

"Ah, Bianca, come in!" said Madame cheerfully, as she opened the door. Head down, Bianca accepted the invitation to enter the office and sit down. The headmistress studied Bianca intently. She made her way back to her desk and folded her hands in front of her.

"I've asked you to come here for a special reason, Bianca," she began, coming straight to the point. "Well, actually for more than one reason, but I hope I can explain the first quickly. Your roommate—Caitlin—has brought to my attention that there is some friction between you and some of the older students."

Bianca's eyes opened wide in disbelief.

"Before you get annoyed with Caitlin—yes, she told me. As you know, I asked her to keep her eye on you, to make sure you're settling in all right."

"By telling you things about me behind my back?"

"At our school, it's customary for the older students to watch out for the new ones." Madame insisted. "Caitlin was worried about you, that's all. I understand you believe someone stole your papers in the library?"

Bianca tried to sink lower in her chair. "I'm missing two pages of notes," she admitted hesitantly.

"And what makes you suspect that it was members of the Wolves?"

Bianca was speechless. Caitlin had really spilled the beans. Finally she cleared her throat.

"Not really suspect," she said, "I just have the feeling that the Wolves don't particularly like me, that's all." Had she said that carefully enough?

Madame Lalonde stood up and went to the window. There was a brief pause. Bianca caught herself nervously kneading her fingers again. For a moment she was tempted to tell Madame everything—about Sylvie's warning, the nightmares, and her suspicion that Annette Durlain's death was not an accident. But she knew how it would sound. Joaquim's words echoed again. But perhaps the headmistress would believe her. She swallowed hard and searched for the right words.

"Basically, I believe that everyone is responsible for choosing her own way." Madame spoke again, and Bianca had to listen. "That means too that everyone looks after her own affairs and is aware that classes at this school can be somewhat harder. Later, at university, or working in a big firm or somewhere, you'll find that the Europa International School has prepared you well for professional life and the … pitfalls of a career."

Bianca closed her mouth again. Sylvie was right. Madame was tougher and less compassionate than she seemed—but also more successful and clear-sighted. Right now Bianca would have given anything to please her and to satisfy the school's demands.

"Regardless," continued Madame, "we'll look into the matter: question students, find out who was in the library at that time, speak to the staff…"

"No," said Bianca in a firm voice. "No—it was my mistake. Next time I'll watch out for my belongings better."

The appreciative smile that Madame gave her made her feel like she had just been knighted.

"Good. So that's that," said the headmistress. "Let's get to the second point." With an energetic motion she opened a drawer, took out a folder, and laid it on the desk so that Bianca could see the cover page.

"Your history test, marked," said Madame. "Look at it at your leisure."

Bianca stood up and picked up the folder. Through the transparent cover the mark looked like 30 percent. That must be a trick of the light! Incredulously Bianca turned back the cover. It was no trick. Bianca read her name at the side and ran her eye over the first few lines of the test. It was her close handwriting, rather too small—but the answers were not the ones she remembered writing. Errors had crept in, and she had obviously completely missed two questions, although she was sure that she had read them all carefully. She continued to leaf through. Every red mark was like a physical blow. She even found the place where she had made a mistake and had crossed out the first letter of the line. It was clearly her writing. Was she going mad?

"Well?" asked Madame Lalonde.

"I... I don't know. Yesterday I thought..."

Bianca's throat felt as if a hand was closing around it. Just don't cry! Not now! If she admitted now that she was going mad, she'd be put on the next train and sent home, that was certain. And nothing could be worse than having to go home.

Madame Lalonde sighed and suddenly looked tired. She pinched the base of her nose, as if trying to get rid of a headache.

"As you can imagine, it isn't my decision alone whether you stay at this school," she said quietly. "And only the best can stay here. You may be a genius in math—but if you don't make more effort in the other subjects, it won't matter."

"I know."

"However, you still have the chance to make up for this poor result on the next two tests," continued Madame. "The next couple of weeks will be quieter for you anyway, since the senior classes are writing their exams. Use this time to catch up on what you have missed. I hope you will make more effort in future. If there is some other reason you are not able to concentrate on studying for these exams, you must tell me. You know I really want you to stay."

The intimacy between them was suddenly back. Bianca felt as if a warm hand was stroking her hair; it was a strange feeling that confused her and at the same time gave her strength.

"I believe you are very talented, Bianca. You have a scholarship from the Maddalina of Trenta Foundation—make something of it!"

Bianca felt a little guilty when her mother's tired, washed-out face flashed before her. She would never have encouraged her like this. She had not been happy that Bianca was going to a boarding school—even at their parting she had hardly said a word. And during the whole journey to the school, Bianca had been expecting her phone to ring, but it had remained silent, dead, like the unspoken words between them.

"But, actually, I called you in because of something quite different," said Madame. "As you know, here at the Europa International School we make use of our contacts with the university as early as possible. We offer students who are already interested in a particular field of study a very special program. They can work with professors in their chosen area in a mentoring project for a period of eight weeks. That means they are introduced early to the basics of their future field of study and can get a real sense of what it entails. At the end of the project they receive a comprehensive evaluation from their mentor." Her smile became wider. "I was able to persuade Dr. Hasenberg that you should approach him regarding such a project. Provided, of course, that your average improves—but I have no doubt in that regard. What do you think?"

Bianca took a breath and nodded, dazed.

"Wonderful!" cried Madame. "Then write this down: Thursday, 5 p.m. You know where Dr. Hasenberg's office is? He'll be expecting you."

BIANCA HAD ONLY JUST GOT BACK to her room when there was a knock at the adjoining door. Caitlin could not hide her feelings. Her cheeks burned as she attempted an apologetic smile.

"Well, well, Sherlock Holmes in person," said Bianca coldly.

Caitlin's smile turned into a rueful grimace. "I'm sorry, Bianca—I didn't think Madame would make such a big deal of it."

"How dare you tell anyone of my private affairs?"

Caitlin's face went even redder. "Madame caught me and asked me all sorts of questions."

"Do you have any idea what you've done to me? I look like a hysterical idiot!"

"She really pumped me for information," insisted Caitlin. "But she could have asked anyone. Take a good look at yourself, Bianca. Obviously the business of the dead woman took more out of you than you realize. Plus, I'm always having to make excuses for you to your parents when they call. What's that all about?"

"I don't want to talk about it," snapped Bianca. "That's the last time I'll ever trust you! I'll never tell you anything ever again." She grabbed her jacket and stormed past the flabbergasted Caitlin into the hallway. Head down, she hurried down the stairs. As she walked, she looked at her watch—if she hurried, she would just catch the bus into town. All she wanted was to get away from here! She ran around the corner—and crashed right into Jan. With a loud clatter his bag fell the ground. Screwdrivers and bits of metal poured out onto the stone floor. Jan went deathly pale at the sight of the metal entrails of his bag.

He turned on her. "Why don't you watch where you're going?"

"I could ask you the same thing. I'm trying to catch the bus."

He cursed and bent down to quickly pick up his equipment. Reluctantly, Bianca helped him gather his things. She held up a little pair of pliers.

"Give them to me!" he said through gritted teeth. "You don't want to miss your bus. I'll deal with this."

Bianca nodded and jumped up. She left the school building at a run, gravel spraying at every step. She headed toward the bus stop and did not stop to catch her breath until the school grounds were far behind her. The running felt good. As she neared the bus stop, however, she saw the bus driving away around the bend. Too bad. Feeling uneasy, she looked back. Glass sparkled in the sun. The building crouched there as if lying in wait. The elegantly curved crossbeams of the facade looked like a malicious grin. Her cell phone rang. Caitlin's number lit up on the display. Reluctantly she turned it off. On a whim, she decided to walk into town. Somewhere between two and three miles—she could manage that.

But soon after she set out it started to drizzle. Bianca hunched her shoulders and walked as fast as she could. Cars zoomed past her, and then a motorcycle whipped by. Bianca saw it slow down just ahead of her and then accelerate again. It disappeared around the bend with a loud roar.

Nearly an hour later she was there. The road led to a residential district on the outskirts, and a local bus came along, which she took into the town center. The town was quaint: a square in the middle, a medieval pillar commemorating the plague, a bit of unspoiled old town, with ever more modern areas surrounding it like the growth rings of a tree. The most impressive things were St. George's Church and the huge university buildings, which loomed near the square.

The rain had stopped, and in the sun of early summer the medieval facades of the houses were glowing like an old painting. Tourists sat in the cafés, their cameras on the empty seats beside them. Students were cycling or ambling toward the university for afternoon lectures, knapsacks on their shoulders. Bianca followed a group of them along the little street to the market square, stopped to contemplate the gentle face of Mary atop the medieval pillar, and then hurried to catch up. Two streets later they were at the university. Bianca stood still and watched them crossing the square. A broad staircase led to the entrance. Longingly Bianca watched the students disappear through the heavy wooden door. If she did not manage to improve her marks, this door would be closed to her. A feeling of loss hit her, although nothing had changed yet.

A metallic flicking sound brought her back to reality. She looked to her right. A few feet away stood Leatherjacket, lighting a cigarette. A flurry of wind blew through his hair and tugged at the turned-up collar of his leather jacket. A black crash helmet was atop his knapsack, which was standing on the ground.

"Hello, Snow White." Without a word she turned and ran back the way she had come. At the end of the market square she looked back. He was not following her. When she reached the center of town, she was still almost running, her hands balled into fists in her jacket pockets.

He was standing, breathing hard, in front of one of the cafés, waiting for her. For a moment she was confused. Had he flown? Looking sheepish, he held up his hand.

“Hey, I’m sorry about that,” he said. “That was pretty stupid of me. I didn’t mean to scare you.”

“How did you...”

“... get here? Short cut. Through Pelargus Alley. My student residence is there—it’s quicker than going the long way around via the market square. I thought you were going back to the bus.”

For a while they looked at each other. Bianca noticed that he had gray-blue eyes and he looked as if he hadn’t seen too much sun recently.

“My name’s Nicholas,” he said finally. “Nicholas Varkonyi.”

“You’ve been spying on me—I saw you at the school.”

He smiled nervously and shrugged his shoulders. He couldn’t hide his feelings any better than Caitlin. With this observation, some of Bianca’s confidence returned.

“That’s right,” he said. “I’ve been spying on you, because—I have to talk to you, please.”

“You’re one of the Wolves, right?” she said challengingly.

He frowned. “Interesting you should say that.” He looked around a little too casually. “Can I buy you a cup of coffee? I don’t want to discuss this sort of thing out in the open. La Bête is over there.” With an ironic smile he added: “There are lots of people in there. And it has windows, too.”

Bianca still hesitated, but when a few raindrops fell on her face, she gave in. She reached into her jacket pocket, though, and turned her cell phone back on.

Someone had gone to great lengths to furnish the café in the style of the old black and white movies. Grainy photos of movie stars hung larger than life above black lacquered tables. In the central picture a prince with a cat-like predator’s head was depicted in front of a fairy-tale backdrop. In a niche hung copper engravings of sea monsters, werewolves, and flying fiends. Nervously, Bianca sat down and waited. She did not take off her jacket and shook her head when Nicholas asked her if she wanted to order anything. His nervousness was infectious. Funnily enough, she felt as if she were on a first date with someone who did not know how to impress her. His movements were precise, but agitated. With a practiced gesture he shook a cigarette out of the pack and, like a magician, let it skip over his fingers before lighting it.

"Do you have to do that?" asked Bianca.

He looked at her blankly, and then to her surprise promptly took the cigarette and stubbed it out in the ashtray in silence. The paper tube burst, and tobacco trickled out of it.

"So, what do you want?" she asked.

Nicholas took a deep breath and moistened his lips. "First I'll answer your other question—no, I'm not one of the Wolves. I'm a student here."

"You look pretty young for a student."

"Is eighteen too young?"

"That depends—did you graduate early from the Europa International School?"

"What do you mean?"

"Well, they graduate a year early there—and because of the optional afternoon seminars, you can take an assessment exam when you start university and skip the introductory courses. It saves time."

"No. I've got nothing to do with your school. I'm new here in town, like you." He hesitated before continuing, choosing his words carefully. "I don't exactly know where to start. Your notes disappear, books go missing, and funnily enough, you're always the one who gets the wrong information. Sometimes tests you've written disappear, and your name vanishes from a sign-up list. Does that sound familiar to you at all?"

Bianca folded her arms and leaned back.

"That's what they're doing to me, anyway," added Nicholas. "I don't know about you, but I'm just waiting for the trip wires on the stairs."

"It sounds familiar," admitted Bianca after a while.

Nicholas's face seemed to light up with relief.

"But what are the Wolves doing at the university?" asked Bianca skeptically.

"A lot of Europa students go on to attend this university, as you know. If they were members of the Wolves when they were at the school, they stay in the society while they're at university."

"I see. And what do you want from me?"

He hesitated, as if searching for the right words.

"Well," he began finally. "I thought we could form a sort of self-help group—and do a bit of research. But I'm not a student at the school and have no access to the Wolves' notes."

"And you're looking for them at night in the visitors' parking lot?"

He looked at her blankly. "I have no idea what you're talking about," he said. Bianca gave him a suspicious look and did not reply.

"So, are you in?" asked Nicholas after a pause.

"Do I look like someone who snoops around and puts her graduation at risk? No way! Find someone else!"

She was about to get up when he grabbed her wrist. His fingers were cold. "You don't seem to realize that you'll definitely ruin your graduation if you keep walking into their traps. They want you out—just like they want me out. And they're serious."

He reached into his knapsack, took out a book, and threw it down on the table. "I heard you were looking for a book about saints."

Bianca sank back down onto the chair. She had to make an effort to take the book and look under the letter "A." The portrait of Saint Apollonia looked up at her—with Bianca's hair. Even the underlining below the words was still there.

"A fairly clear threat," said Nicholas. "But you wouldn't be able to prove anything. There was no book about saints listed in the library catalogue, was there? You can never prove anything against them."

"How do you know that?" whispered Bianca. "And you knew that they call me Snow White."

"Oh," he said, leaning back. "No magic there. It was actually supposed to be a joke." Surprised, she saw that he was blushing slightly. "Well, you have such fair skin. And with that black hair, too..."

"Don't lie to me," hissed Bianca. "How do you know about the book?"

"Someone told me."

"Who?"

He put up his hand defensively. "Believe it or not—the story got around."

"And where did you get the book?"

"I simply looked in the theological department." Nicholas smiled and drummed his fingers against the table. But his smile faded. "You don't trust me."

"Just before the book surfaced, I saw you in front of the library. Who's to say you didn't put the book there yourself?"

"No one," he replied. "You only have my word. I was looking for you that day in the library, because I wanted to talk to you. You see, there's something else."

He leaned forward. "When I was on the train on the way here, somebody told me the story about how the Wolves threw someone into the river."

"I know that story. So?"

"It really happened, nineteen years ago. It was a student—and he drowned."

"What?"

"An accident," Nicholas continued quietly. "If you want to believe that. Anyway, they were never held responsible for it. No one was accused. Strange, don't you think? And I'll tell you something else. It was you who found the dead woman a month ago, wasn't it?"

Bianca stiffened.

"That's right."

"Do you believe that Annette Durlain's death was an accident?"

Suddenly Bianca's mouth was so dry that she could hardly get out her answer. She looked directly into Nicholas's eyes. "No," she replied.

He half smiled and then nodded. "Me neither. Did you notice anything? Anything at all—was there any sign of an injury?"

"Just read last week's paper. There's more in it than I know about her. Why?"

He played with his lighter. "Promise you won't blab? The story's a bit—delicate. If it comes out that I've talked, I'm toast. You won't tell anyone? Deal?" He held out his hand to her.

Bianca wavered, but eventually shook his hand.

"Good," he said, putting his fingertips together like a professor. "Officially she stumbled and fell downstairs—an accident. And I also know the story about the crazies who are so fascinated with witches they want to spend a night beside the witch's robe.

It might even be true. But there's one detail that could turn the whole thing around."

"She didn't break her neck?"

"Oh yes, she did. Only… she had this weird wound."

"A wound—so what? That doesn't prove anything."

"It happened after her death. Not very smart, huh?"

Bianca held her breath. She felt as if the café was rocking. The movie monsters seemed to be smirking.

"How do you know that?"

He pointed at his chest.

"Medical student," he said. "Orderly at the Institute of Forensic Medicine, reports lying around, gossip in the waiting rooms."

"You go snooping in reports that are none of your business?"

"No, I photocopy the reports."

There was a short pause, and Bianca suddenly felt cold. Up until now, her suspicions had only been a game in her own mind, but now it was becoming frighteningly real. Could it really be murder?

"The Wolves," she said quietly. And mentally added: Or Nemec?

"Do you think it's possible that they have something to do with it?" Nicholas asked.

"They're students. Why would they kill someone?"

"To get rid of witnesses? Greed? Or revenge? It might have been a commission for someone else. We'll figure it out. So, are you in?"

Bianca shook her head and jumped up.

"Where are you going?"

"Away from here!" she replied sharply.

"What's wrong? Was it something I said?"

"You have to go to the police!"

"I don't trust them. Didn't you read what it said in the paper? No one else was involved!"

"Ever heard of undercover investigations? Quite likely the police have known about your discovery for ages and just want to give the murderer a false sense of security."

Nicholas held up his hands in a conciliatory gesture. "Fine, end of conversation. But please take time to think about it. At the university there's no documentation on the Wolves, and I don't have access to the documents at Europa."

"I won't think about it at all—I'm leaving."

"Can I call you? Give me some way to contact you—the school number, or whatever you like."

"No."

He tore a piece off the cigarette pack, scribbled something on it, and pushed the scrap over to her.

"My cell number. Please just take it with you, OK? Just in case."

STIGMA DIABOLICUM

THE WHOLE CLASS was suffering while Mrs. Catalon tried to scratch out a particularly beautiful diagram on the board with a squeaky piece of chalk. Today Bianca was finding it more difficult than usual to follow Mrs. Catalon's explanations. For the first time in weeks she felt wide awake again. The heavy fog that had wrapped itself around her thoughts had disappeared. With her pen she scribbled little circles and arrows in the margin of her notebook. Simon Nemec had been weeping—would a murderer weep for his victim? Or was he crying because he had known Annette Durlain? And Annette Durlain—was there really a connection between her and the Wolves? Bianca could hardly wait for the bell to ring for lunch break.

The few students who came from the town and lived at home jumped onto their bikes and rode away, not to return until just before three o'clock for afternoon classes.

Bianca ran to the library building. She was in luck—the computer stations were free; only a few of the older students, preparing to write their first final exam with Caitlin in three days, were scattered around the room, hunched over their notes. Bianca sat down at a computer and logged on. It took forever until she could enter her keywords into the search engine: "Simon Nemec." Not a single hit. Annette Durlain did not exist on the Internet either—not even on the French pages when she added "Brest" to the search. Under "Joaquim Almán" there were just the results and tables from sports tournaments, but Bianca did find several pages for a certain J. Almán. She called up the picture search function and waited. Three pictures appeared—and Bianca immediately knew it was Joaquim's father. Sure, he was balding and wore round glasses, but the facial expression, the mouth, and the eyes were identical. The photos all came from charitable institutions he was involved with, but none of the articles mentioned how he actually earned his money. Bianca printed out a few pages, then called up the library's online catalogue and entered "Maddalina of Trenta." That got 28 hits, of which she was immediately able to eliminate 24. The last four were interesting, though: printed copies of the convent chronicle, as well as the complete records of the witch trial, a short history of the school—not much more than a booklet, written in 1961—and also an essay about Saint Belverina. Something, at least. Under keywords for the town chronicle she found only current directories and school yearbooks. Bianca noted down the location of the books and started a new search. Using the search word "Wolves" she got 159 hits in the biology department. Once more she limited her search, combining it with concepts like "student association," "society," "Middle Ages," the name of the town—and landed on a single book. It was the same book, the one that told the history of the school. With a sigh of relief, she shut down the program and looked at her watch. She still had time. Caitlin's fellow sufferers hardly looked up as Bianca went over to the checkout desk.

"I'd like to see these, please," she said to the library aide behind the counter, a student whose hair shone with a harsh orange tone. She was probably earning a bit of extra cash by working in the library. "N. Kuhlmann" was printed on the badge on her shirt collar. Wrinkling her brow, she studied the information Bianca had scribbled in her notebook.

"If that's an M and this scrawl here is 49, then we have the book in the stockroom. We only let out books like that when there's a reason for it. What do you need it for?"

"History essay," lied Bianca without hesitation. She bit her lip. Would it work?

"Oh, I see." The student smiled. "You should have said that right away. Then I need a note from your teacher. Do you have it with you?"

Bianca gulped and shook her head. "I wanted to suggest the topic and do a bit of research ahead of time. I'll get the note tomorrow and bring it in."

N. Kuhlmann frowned and looked searchingly at Bianca. "You're the new girl in tenth grade, aren't you? The one sharing a room with Caitlin O'Connell?"

Bianca nodded and prepared herself for the next question. Instead, the girl pushed a form over to her. "Here, fill the card out. I'll get the book for you."

"Thanks," said Bianca, surprised. "I'll bring the note tomorrow, then..."

The student stood up and waved her hand dismissively. "Don't bother," she said. "As long as it's OK with Madame, then it's fine with me."

THE CONVENT CHRONICLE had been photocopied page by page—gray shadows indicated that the original had been yellowed or dirty. Only a few pages were reproduced in color. Black writing ran over a yellowish-brown background, and from time to time there was a page with splendidly illustrated initial letters. With an effort Bianca could decipher quite well the lines composed in German. In a footnote, a well-meaning translator had translated the Latin lines into clumsy German. Unfortunately the writing was so small that within half an hour Bianca's neck was so stiff it felt as if it was carved out of wood.

The convent had been home to the order for nearly 150 years. It was named for Saint Belverina. Bianca already knew her picture from the museum. "Belverina was carried off from her home in England by the Vikings and sold to the court of the king of Neustrien as a slave in 641," Bianca read. "Held in high esteem for her wisdom, she rose quickly to high rank and was particularly fond of the children of the court. After the king's death, Belverina became advisor to the ten-year-old heir to the throne. She acquired great wealth, and with it she endowed orphanages and founded convents. Around 675 she was cruelly murdered following a conspiracy by the aristocracy." The description went on to say that Saint Belverina was considered to be the patron saint of children up to that day. A dog sat next to her as a symbol of loyalty. Well, that was interesting, but it didn't really give her anything to go on. The dog had little to do with a wolf: in the picture it looked far more like a deer sitting on its haunches. A few pages further on, Bianca discovered inventories relating to the convent's housekeeping. At the time of the witch trial, eleven women had been living in the convent. The last entry was made in February of 1651; on the following pages the translator had written a summary of the witch trial. Bianca snapped the book shut and looked at the clock. Ten to two. If she wanted to finish her physics homework before afternoon classes, she'd better hurry.

She bent over her knapsack and packed up her books. Only now did she notice how quiet the library had become. No more rustling of paper, no clearing of throats, no footsteps. Bianca looked up and froze. Joaquim was standing in front of her. All the other students had already left. Even the student at the checkout desk was gone.

"Hello, Bianca," said Joaquim. His smile was no warmer than a snowball.

"Congratulations," she replied. "You've managed to memorize my name after all." She hoped he could not hear her heart hammering with fear. "Where are your gorillas?" she asked, as the pause grew longer.

His eyes had the warm color of dark amber—a strange contrast to his harsh manner. He was pale and looked overtired. "Who do you think you are?" he said quietly.

"Who do you guys think you are?" she returned.

"Good students," he answered sharply. "And a loser like you simply comes along and snatches up a mentoring project. Do you know that you usually have to be in your second year at the school to get one? And then only with an average of at least 80 percent."

"Who told you about it?" she replied calmly.

"Hasenberg," came the answer. "He's my mentor. That is—he was, until yesterday."

Bianca was dumbfounded.

Joaquim looked at her with hatred, his lips pinched.

"It wasn't my idea," she protested. "I didn't know anything about the rules."

"I won't let anyone stand in my way."

"Right. And the best way to manage that is to steal my notes. Very clever, Joaquim."

"Did you tell Madame that bullshit?" he hissed. "I'm beginning to understand! You lying bitch!"

"Hey, watch what you're saying!"

He lowered his voice to a warning whisper. "Oh, I'm really frightened." He took a step forward and stood so close to her that she had to tilt her head back to look into his eyes. "Are you going to go straight back to Madame and cry on her shoulder?"

Bianca drew back, bumping painfully into the edge of the table.

"Careful," he said. "Something might happen to you."

"I wouldn't be the first," she said with an effort.

"And that alone should make you think," he replied amiably.

"What do you intend to do? Beat me up like Sylvie?"

Her question did not disconcert him at all. Amused, he half smiled.

"We don't beat people up. At most we remind people of their proper place."

"Leave me alone!" she hissed, pulling away from him. With all her strength she hit him with her knapsack full of books. He groaned, and his hand shot forward, but Bianca ducked under his grasp and ran. In the passageway in front of the door she nearly crashed into the aide, who sprang aside with a shocked cry.

From the painful throbbing in her jaw, Bianca realized that she had been gritting her teeth the whole time. She tore open the door and dashed toward the stairs. From the floor below her came the subdued murmur of voices. Just the big staircase, then she would be among people! A blow came from the side, knocking her legs from under her. While she was still falling, she had the sudden thought that it could not have been Joaquim. The stairs flew toward her. Everything seemed to be happening in slow motion—she felt as if she was seeing with Annette Durlain's eyes: she was aware of every single step and could see with absolute clarity that any moment now she would fall down the stairs. Something wrenched her shoulder painfully and pulled her back, then two arms wrapped themselves around her and dragged her into the alcove by the stairs.

"That nearly went wrong, Snow White," said Tanja mockingly.

Dazed, Bianca looked up at her. Her shoulder still hurt—Tanja had twisted her arm behind her back. A practice stick pressed against her throat.

"Turn down the project!" said Tanja softly and very clearly. "If you don't, I'll make sure you do. And I guarantee you one thing: it'll hurt."

"You won't get away with this!" Bianca said through gritted teeth.

"Wanna bet?" replied Tanja.

A whistle pierced the air. Joaquim appeared, out of nowhere. The color drained from his face when he saw Bianca at the top of the stairs. Suddenly he just looked helpless and frightened.

"That's enough," he said hoarsely. "Let her go."

Abruptly Tanja loosened her grip and removed the stick. As quickly as she could, Bianca crawled away from the stairs; not until she felt the solid wall did she begin to stand up slowly. Joaquim and Tanja stood face to face.

"You're going too far," he hissed at her. The girl stared at him, not comprehending.

"But you said... Why...?" There was disappointment in her voice. All at once Bianca had the impression that she could see right through Tanja. What else might she do for Joaquim?

"Because," came the gruff answer. "Leave her alone, OK?" Not deigning to look at Bianca, he turned around and walked away, his shoulders seeming to bear a great weight.

Tanja gave Bianca a look that was hurt and vindictive in equal measure. She lowered her voice to a whisper. "Just don't get any silly ideas. No one will believe you."

"Madame will!"

"Madame needs money. Joaquim's father isn't just the chairman of the school foundation. He *is* the foundation. What do you think is more important to her—her school or someone like you? Who are you, Bianca? Some loopy bastard whose parents threw her away like garbage?"

She picked up the other practice sticks and hurried after Joaquim. Bianca watched her go, stunned. A wave of nausea hit her. For a moment she thought she was actually going to throw up. She sank to the ground, wrapped her arms around her knees, and sat there, trembling.

FOR THE FIRST TIME she was glad that Caitlin was not there. It was easier to cry when no one was in the next room. Bianca was freezing, although it was nearly 90 degrees outside. It was Tanja's last words that had hurt the most. How did she know so much about Bianca? With damp fingers she searched the side pocket of her knapsack. Finally her fingers found the soft torn edge of the cardboard. There it was—Nicholas's number, scribbled down on a bit of his cigarette pack. Bianca clasped the scrap in her hand. Should she call him after all? In one bound she leaped up, locked the door and the adjoining door to Caitlin's room, leaving the key in it. The phone rang exactly eight times before someone picked up.

"Varkonyi."

Bianca hesitated. "Hello," she said finally.

"Bianca?" His delight at getting her call made her feel good. "That's... to be honest, I didn't think you'd call!"

"I didn't either, until just now. Where are you?"

"Pelargus student residence, in the kitchen. My job doesn't begin till four. And where are you?"

She hesitated. "I just got back from the library," she said vaguely. There was a pause.

"And?"

"Nothing there about the... Wolves. But I'll keep looking."

"I see." Another pause. "Bianca—is everything all right?"

Bianca took a deep breath. For a moment she was tempted to tell him everything, but then she swallowed and forced herself to speak calmly. "Sure. Nicholas, you asked me yesterday if I could imagine that the Wolves could have had anything to do with Annette Durlain's death."

He said nothing.

"Well," she continued. "I can imagine it—very clearly."

She heard a click in the background and imagined Nicholas playing nervously with his lighter.

"Bianca?"

"Hmm?"

"If anything happens, call me—I can come to the school any time."

"That's not necessary."

"Are you sure? Yesterday you didn't sound as if you had a

cold. Or as if you'd been crying. Did something happen?"

"Listen, Nicholas, I don't need a protector. I'll get the information for you—but stay out of my business, OK?"

"And you listen to me," he replied. "I'm no psychologist, but I don't have to be, to see what you're like. You want to do everything alone—heaven forbid anyone should help you! Isn't that right?"

"None of your business, Mr. Freud." Furious, she hung up. All the same, she felt a little better.

SHORTLY BEFORE MIDNIGHT the light in Caitlin's room finally went out. Bianca waited another half hour, then crept to the adjoining door. She stuffed her bedspread into the gap under the door and sat down at her desk. The light from her bedside table lamp illuminated a yellow moss rose, a gesture of reconciliation from Caitlin. In the silence, the rustling of the pages of the chronicle was so loud that she was sure Caitlin would wake up.

It was all over quickly. From the first accusation to the point when the last little heap of human ashes had blown away and the convent had become known as a place to be avoided—a place of the Devil—just about three months had passed in 1651. Nevertheless the "witch police" had enough time to do their work thoroughly. It had all begun when the novice Maria and two of the older orphan children had been accused of witchcraft. It was said that they used magic to make it rain, ruined the harvest, and visited a plague of mice upon the mill after a dispute with the miller.

Maddalina of Trenta, Regina Maria Sängerin, a deputy prioress by the name of Katharina, and other nuns were on the second list. The accusation quickly spread to the convent's employees—the gardener Hans Haber, a cowherd called Georg Kastellus, and others in the convent's service, such as Theophrast Mittenmann and Bernd Gerber Halgfuss. All together twenty-four people had been arrested and charged, of whom six were "witches' children," boys from the orphanage that was attached to the convent. At the "witch trials" the chronicler had apparently let his imagination be his inspiration:

...Carried Out the Old Familiar Witch Trial with Regina Maria Sängerin, in Accordance with which She was Thrown into the Water with Bound Hands and Feet, Whereupon she Floated like Balsa Wood, in Addition Hildebranter Klara was Put upon a Large Scale, at Which it was Remarkable that this Big, Fat Woman Weigh'd Less than an Ounce

Bianca pulled her notebook out from under the book and noted down: "water trial—drowned student?"

The most extensive account given by the clerk documenting the proceedings was that of the abbess's interrogation. The prosecution and questioning of the six "witches' sons" was also documented most meticulously. They were accused of using magic to cause harm and of contributing to the desecration of the communion bread.

...the Millers Daughter was Infected and Lam'd by the Witches Children Standing Accus'd.

Reference was made to a "stigma diabolicum" being tested on one occasion. The end was the same for all the Belverina nuns, the convent's staff, and the orphan children:

...and All Witches and Conspirators will Receive Eternal Fire for Their Sins.

Regina Maria Sängerin and the fat Hildebranter Klara were the first to be chained to the stakes in the pyre. The public celebrations went on for more than two weeks. The last one was the "witch queen," Maddalina of Trenta, who met her death in the courtyard of her own convent, before the eyes of those who a few weeks before had been her friends and acquaintances. The documentation of the case ended with the last of the clerk's notes:

> *...When They Examined Her Cell, They Found a Robe of Fur, Which She was Wont to Wear When Going Out to Her Customary Witches' Dance.*

Bianca stopped dead. A robe of fur—that did not fit. Except for this detail, it was a classic trial, and if you discounted the over-exuberant imagination of its author, it seemed almost impersonal. Bianca leafed back and skimmed each page again. She saw again the words "stigma diabolicum." To be sure of the meaning, she read the explanation in the footnote: "A mark, usually in the form of a birthmark, that the Devil makes on the body of a witch." In Maddalina of Trenta's case, the devil's mark had been low on her right hip. Bianca looked up from the book to her alarm clock. Half past one.

Despite the late hour, Nicholas picked up at the first ring. His voice sounded breathless, as if he had been sitting beside his cell phone the whole time, waiting for the call.

"Nicholas?"

"Yes!"

"We have to meet. Preferably first thing."

"Sure." He sounded infinitely relieved. "Have you found something?"

"A stigma diabolicum," she said.

THE EXECUTIONER'S SWORD

SHE RECOGNIZED HIM RIGHT AWAY through the café window, despite the distance. The tension in his posture made him stand out, even without his leather jacket. Suddenly she was simply happy he was there. Today he was wearing a black T-shirt that emphasized his thinness. His cigarette smoke danced in the slanting rays of the afternoon sun. Except for Nicholas and an older lady reading the paper, La Bête was empty. Most people were sitting in the ice-cream parlors in the market square. Tourists crowded around a tour guide like a swarm of bees around its queen, turning their heads respectfully toward the pillar and to the church tower, looking for all the world like a well-rehearsed ballet corps. Nicholas seemed to sense that someone was approaching: he looked round before Bianca could call out to him. He quickly stubbed out his cigarette in the ashtray and stood up.

"Hello! Thanks for coming."

They shook hands formally and sat down. For a few uncomfortable seconds they just looked at each other. Nicholas's eyes were like a stormy sky.

"You don't look as though you've had much sleep," he remarked.

"Nor you," she returned. For a moment she was tempted to tell him about the incident on the stairs.

"Anything new on your end?" she asked instead.

"Yesterday my anatomy books disappeared without a trace and they have no record of my registration for a seminar." He swore. "That means I might lose a semester."

"Do you think they're watching us right now?"

She could tell by looking at him that he felt uncomfortable sitting there—carefully he looked around and shook his head.

"It doesn't look like it right now. Come a bit closer!"

She slid her chair closer to his, so they could talk without being overheard. The clerk behind the counter smiled to herself as she watched the couple whispering. Sitting so close to someone was very unusual for Bianca. Suddenly she realized how much she had kept her distance from the people around her in the last few weeks. Nicholas's hair smelled of shampoo, and a blond strand fell over his brow.

"Stigma diabolicum," he whispered. "What's that all about?"

"Just a guess. Maddalina of Trenta had a birthmark. And you said the dead woman in the library had a strange wound?" She leaned further forward. "Did the autopsy report say exactly where this wound was?"

Slowly he let his hand slide to his right side, indicating a spot just below where his belt sat on his hipbone. Bianca nodded. "Just like Maddalina!" she whispered. "I don't know the shape of her birthmark, but do you think it could have been a brand, a tattoo, or something like that, rather than a birthmark? Let's assume that the dead woman had the same mark as Maddalina of Trenta. Then her murderer could have removed the piece of skin so that no one would know she had belonged to a... group."

Nicholas had turned pale. Bianca said nothing as he took out a cigarette with a nervous gesture. He forgot to light it, however.

"Then brace yourself," he said. "Because I found something out, too—the autopsy report has disappeared."

"What?"

"I wanted to copy it today—and then I saw that it had been changed. There's nothing in there about a missing piece of skin any more. Just her broken neck and a few scrapes. The police aren't investigating it any more, Bianca. The case is closed—officially, it was an accident." In Nicholas's eyes the café window was reflected as a light-colored rectangle, its sides arched outward. "That means," he continued, "that there may be more people involved—a doctor, or even several doctors, who are hushing up a murder. Maybe even the doctor I work for."

Bianca watched his hands as he played with the cigarette, twisting and twirling it, until he finally put it back into the pack. "Let's go," she said quietly.

A little later they were walking through the town park. Some students had strung a volleyball net between two trees and were trading volleys vigorously. Bianca and Nicholas crossed the lawn in silence and sat down on the park bench by the duck pond. Bianca pulled her knees to her chin and stared at the mirror-like surface of the water.

"The student who drowned," she said after a while. "His death may be connected with the witch trial. In the record there's an account of a trial by water. It could be a ritual—maybe a punishment, or even a test of courage that got out of hand. We have to get a list of members of the Wolves. All the names listed since the society was founded. If we look hard enough, I bet we'll find the name Annette Durlain. The student associations must have all the old yearbooks and photos in their meeting rooms..."

"Don't waste your time," Nicholas interrupted her. "They don't have meeting rooms. And no local bar, either, where the Wolves have a regular table. They never use a room, not even the Carnival Association. There are just the minutes of meetings in the Oliver O'Deen room below the student cafeteria, where the upcoming training plans are discussed, and the cost of costumes and new flags for their part in the town's medieval festival, but strangely enough, none of the Wolves have actually met there at those times." He leaned back. "At least, if you can believe the schedule by the cafeteria, where the university theatre group books the room for its rehearsals, too. Unless, of course, the Wolves held their last official meeting with a play rehearsal going on in the background."

"So, no meeting room," said Bianca. "No information in the school library or at the university, no history. Just those dumb costume games. They make fools of people with their Carnival Association nonsense. And I have a feeling that this isn't just about the Wolves. There's something else. Something... something I don't get..." She had talked herself into such a fury that Nicholas looked at her in astonishment.

"What do you mean?" he asked.

Bianca thought about the phantom, her nightmares, and Simon Nemec weeping.

"I can't describe it exactly," she said evasively. "Something threatening."

Now Nicholas was looking at her so uncertainly that she decided to change the subject, and quickly. "Forget it. Somewhere there must be more information about the Wolves—maybe in the town museum? I've read that there's an archive there." She looked at her watch. "I still have an hour and a half before my afternoon class. What about your lectures?"

Nicholas hesitated. "Well," he said finally, "if we leave right away, it'll be OK."

THE TOWN MUSEUM was next to the old town hall. It was an unprepossessing modern building that looked out of place beside the town hall's half-timbered facade. Bianca and Nicholas pushed past a group of Japanese tourists, who were looking up at the clock in fascination, waiting for the chimes that rang every hour.

In the museum it was cool, and they could smell new stone and fresh paint. The interior rooms looked as though the building had originally been intended as a gallery. Soft light fell through circular skylights of frosted glass. The exhibits were displayed on modern steel and glass structures. There was a section with artifacts from the Bronze Age, Roman coins, and the plaster cast of a horse skeleton. Bianca almost had to run to keep up with Nicholas. Drawings of Celtic warriors and gleaming lance tips flashed by. The coolness felt good, although the sudden temperature change left Bianca dazed.

"That's the way to the Middle Ages and early modern times, over there," whispered Nicholas.

Bianca nodded and followed him through the reproduction of a city gate. At first glance the exhibits looked like those in the Convent Museum. Here too were a monstrance, embroidered altar cloths, and golden goblets for mass.

"At the back there's a model of the original convent," said Nicholas softly. His steps made hardly any sound on the smooth, gray floor. Bianca went from one display case to the next, finding craftsmen's seals and documents, portraits of guild elders, spinning wheels, and a cradle decorated with inlaid silver, which was enthroned like a work of art on a steel pedestal. At the end of the exhibition room she found a small passageway. Obviously the architect wanted to create the atmosphere of a journey of discovery, for the passage came to a dead end that was unlit.

Bianca went closer and squinted to read the text. "Special Exhibition," she read on a poster. "Witches, Hangmen, Torturers—1 March to 31 August." Wondering whether to wait for Nicholas, she looked around, but he was nowhere to be seen. So she entered the passageway alone and went toward the shadowy corner. A worm-eaten door came into view. In front of its square window was an iron railing. Only when Bianca was standing directly in front of it did she realize that it was just a photograph on the white door. Bianca pressed down the handle, entered—and was standing in the middle of a torture chamber. Straw rustled beneath her feet, and the walls were formed of roughly hewn blocks of stone, like castle walls. Imitation torches lit up the room. The glass cases, in which the flickering light was reflected, were the only reminder that this was a museum. Bianca wiped her forehead—despite the cold, she had broken out in a sweat—and looked around. Not all of the exhibits were from this town: some were on loan from areas throughout Europe. The prize of the collection was an angular reclining chair whose seat and back were covered with iron spikes.

Just as Bianca was about to turn away, her glance fell on an exhibit in the corner. It was a jagged sword with a very straight, not too broad blade. To its right hung a yellowed document. Bianca moved closer and read the write-up. The sword had belonged to Johann Georg Feverlin, town executioner until his death in 1654. A small thank-you note indicated that the sword now was part of a private collection and had only been made available to the museum for the duration of this special exhibition. The document said that Johann Georg Feverlin had given evidence of his qualification to be town executioner on 5 September, 1646. The date was interesting—the hangman had lived in the town at exactly Maddalina's time. The name of the family who had lent the sword to the exhibit was, however, not noted. Bianca took out her notebook and wrote down the dates. A few steps on she came across documents that looked familiar to her—that's right, they were parts of the documents that she had read yesterday. Page by page she skimmed through the interrogation records. Nothing new, she established after a while, disappointed. The same sentences, the same sequence of events, the same gaps. Finally she had reached the photograph of the page of the record that lay in front of the witch's robe in the Convent Museum.

> *...He Ask'd Maddalina of Trenta [if she] Her Self had been Qveen of the Witches there [at the Witches Dances] amongst Witch People and Fiends.*

Disappointed, Bianca stood up, tipped her head back and massaged her stiff neck with her right hand. Then she stopped and read the words again. "Fiends," it said. Not "Feends," like at the Convent Museum. As she tried to leaf back through her notebook much too fast, a page tore with a horrible noise. There it was—the sentence she had copied down letter by letter in the school museum. It was identical to the one in the photo—except for the spelling of this one word.

Bianca was so absorbed in comparing the original and the photo that she did not notice at first that there was someone else in the room now. Not until she heard breathing did she press the notebook to her chest and instinctively hide behind the torture chair. The smell of finish restorer and old wood stung her nose.

It was Nicholas, of course. He had buried his hands in his pockets and was looking around with a concerned expression. Bianca cleared her throat and stood up. Nicholas jumped. "Man, so this is where you are!" he said.

Bianca beckoned him to come closer. "Take a look at this!" she whispered, pulling him toward the wall.

Nicholas compared the sentence in the notebook with the photograph several times and whistled softly through his teeth.

"Either the original document at your school is forged, or the document that was photographed is a fake," he confirmed.

"I had the feeling yesterday that the chronicle was incomplete. It all seems too smooth—like a model trial for a textbook on the witch hunts. But in one paragraph it mentions that Maddalina of Trenta had a fur cloak that she supposedly wore when she carried out her devil's rites. That just doesn't fit the picture. I have a feeling that an important part of the documents is missing..."

"...and at the very least, that there are two versions of the interrogation record," said Nicholas, finishing her sentence.

THEY FOUND THE ONLY PICTURES and documents that referred to the Wolves in the "Town History" section. The whole wall was set up like a page from a gigantic family album. The photos were in simple frames and showed the town in different periods, the turn of the century, after the Second World War and in the sixties. Naturally, the manor house had also been photographed—before it had been renovated it had looked like a dark gray temple from a silent movie. In addition, there was a framed list with the names of the people who had made donations to support the restoration of the old buildings and the orphans' cemetery. The cemetery had been protected as a historical monument for nearly fifty years. Among the sponsors, a Dr. Almán was listed—of course, Joaquim's father was an active supporter of the school and surely also of everything belonging to it. Bianca read through the list, name by name, until she came across one at the bottom that she knew only too well.

"Colin Sinclair," she whispered. "That's the detective who questioned me after I found the dead woman."

"That doesn't prove he's connected with the Wolves—it just means he gave money for the restoration. But it could well explain why the investigation was dropped so suddenly."

Nicholas indicated a row of small pictures. They were photos of the town's associations and institutions—the Vintners and the Beautification Society, the group that promoted traditional costumes, and the Music Association. Finally, near the door, there were about a dozen photos of the Wolves. The earliest dated from 1955; in them the costumes looked heavy and roughly sewn. Over the decades the costumes changed, adapting to the fashion of the day. In 1972 the nun's hair was in a topknot and the man wearing the wolf mask had sideburns. The silent faces seemed to smile at Bianca and Nicholas knowingly.

"They look like a harmless Carnival Association," said Bianca, with disappointment.

"Last try," Nicholas murmured.

In the entrance hall the museum employee was bent over her keyboard. She did not notice the two visitors until Nicholas cleared his throat. Fascinated, Bianca eyed a huge wart near the corner of the old lady's mouth.

"My name is Klaus Jehle," said Nicholas. "From the university newspaper, *Attempto*." He pulled out a laminated card. The lady raised her brows, but barely gave the card a glance. "I'm doing some research for an article about the medieval festival," Nicholas continued, "and I'm particularly interested in the history of the Wolves. I didn't find anything about it in the museum." The woman looked at the card intently and then her expression became a little more friendly.

"You won't have much luck here."

"Don't you have archives? You have the original documents of the city library here, don't you?" Regretfully, the lady shook her head and reached for a pen and paper. "We have pretty much nothing on the school history or the Wolves here." She scribbled a couple of names on the paper and searched briefly in the computer before adding the phone number. "The best place to look is the university library—or better still, at the Europa International School. I'll give you a couple of names." She smiled at Nicholas, making the wart wander in the direction of her ear. "Say hello to the lady from Mrs. Nyen. Or you could ask one of the Wolves directly."

"Good idea," said Nicholas without the least hint of irony. "Thanks a lot."

He hid his disappointment well, but Bianca could not resist asking another question.

"Why don't you have any of the original documents?"

Mrs. Nyen's smile became cool. "Well, if you had read the museum's history on the third floor carefully, you would know that, unfortunately, the archive was almost completely destroyed by an electrical fire in 1954. Luckily the school had copies of the convent documents as well as a few original pages of the convent chronicle."

"Thanks very much," said Nicholas, taking the paper. "I'll bring you a copy of the article as soon as the paper comes out."

OUT IN THE LOBBY they were hit by a wave of heat, a taste of what awaited them in the market square.

"Since when is your name Klaus Jehle?" asked Bianca.

"Since the real Klaus, who lives on my floor, lent me his ID. Hey, what's wrong?"

Bianca had come to a halt. She gave Nicholas a suspicious look.

"I just feel less and less sure about what I should believe," she said. "Are you lying to me? You're a journalist, aren't you?"

Nicholas's mouth fell open. "Where were you brought up?" he asked, annoyed. "The gulag? Why are you so suspicious?"

"I just want to know where I stand."

He swore, turned around, and left her standing there. The museum door swung shut in her face. Bianca reached for the steel handle and pushed against the door with all her strength. Relieved, she saw that Nicholas was standing on the steps. He did not look at her as she ran down to him.

"What do you want me to show you?" he shouted at her suddenly. "Passport? Student ID? University registration?"

"No, I just wanted to know..."

He shook his head vigorously. "It'd be nice if you just believed me." With these words he pulled out his wallet and took out a photo.

"I'm not a journalist. If my father had had any say, I'd be a stonemason like him. This is him, in front of his business, in Hemmoor, in northern Germany."

He held a picture out to her. A thin man stood in front of a workshop, smiling into the camera. He had hardly any hair left on his head, yet the similarity was amazing. Nicholas turned the picture over.

"Sandor Varkonyi," it said on the company stamp.

"My family comes from Kecskemét in Hungary. Can you imagine what it costs my father to send me to university here? I'm not going to let the Wolves take that away from me."

"I'm sorry. I just thought..."

"Exactly," replied Nicholas ironically. "You think—that's the problem. You think far too much!"

He put the photo away and studied the piece of paper the lady at the museum had given him.

"Mrs. Klaas—that's the librarian at the university. I talked to her last week, and she couldn't help me. What about this name?" Bianca looked at the paper.

"Natalie Kuhlmann. That's the student who's responsible for the library stockroom. And I've already gone right through that."

"Not much help," remarked Nicholas.

"There's still the hangman."

"What hangman?"

"In the special exhibition there's an executioner's sword. It belonged to the hangman Johann Georg Feverlin. He lived at exactly the time of the Belverina witch hunts." She lowered her voice. "It said on the notice that the sword comes from a private collection. We have to be able to find out who it belongs to—maybe a descendant of the hangman. They might know something about it, or they might have some documents from that time."

A smile flitted over Nicholas's face. He nudged her appreciatively. "Not bad!"

"Do you think the wart lady will give us the address?"

"You can be sure of that!" Nicholas took out his wallet and put the paper into it. When it flopped open, Bianca noticed several large bills.

"Did you win at Bingo?"

Nicholas quickly closed the wallet. "Something like that," he said apologetically. "I cashed a check today. Do you have any idea what a room in the Pelargus residence costs?"

He caught sight of Bianca's watch. "Don't you have to go to class? If you hurry you can catch the next bus."

Bianca slung her knapsack over her shoulder. "We'll talk on the phone!"

"Be careful!" he called after her. "And call me—no matter how late it is. My cell phone's on all the time."

"Same here," she called back.

ENGRAM

THIS PARTICULAR THURSDAY not even Dr. Kalaman could lure her into the realm of probability theory. Unable to concentrate on the lecture, Bianca leafed through her notes. "Sylvie" was underlined twice in the margin. In a few days, when she'd returned to school, Bianca would have to get a hold of her.

Bianca had not seen the other Wolves since the incident on the stairs—and in the evenings she not only locked her door, but also pushed the back of her chair under the door handle.

"What on earth are you doing here?" Caitlin called out, when Bianca came into the room after her afternoon seminar. "Don't you have that appointment with Dr. Hasenberg?"

"Oh, crap!" Bianca turned on her heels and ran. It was two minutes to five when she finally reached the language labs. Taking two stairs at a time, she raced up to the third floor. She ignored the stitch in her side and knocked.

Dr. Hasenberg had light brown curly hair and looked far too young to be a university professor of psychology. Bianca guessed he was barely thirty. "Right on time," he said, pretending not to notice how out of breath she was. "Come in and sit down."

The room was sparsely furnished—the two blue armchairs

could not do justice to what could have been a cozy sitting area. A heavy, black-lacquered bookcase took up almost a whole wall. Behind its shiny glass doors the books looked like the sad inmates of a glass institution. Hasenberg simply did not belong in a room that exuded this aura of sober administration. The door to the next room was ajar, and behind it a secretary was tapping away at a computer.

"Water? Orange juice?"

"No, thanks," said Bianca, trying to breathe normally. Dr. Hasenberg poured himself a glass of water and sat down, facing her, mimicking the way she was sitting. Bianca nearly grinned. Was he copying her posture to make her feel he was trustworthy?

She crossed her legs the other way and folded her arms.

Hasenberg gave a faint smile. "Madame Lalonde tells me you want to take psychology at university?"

Boy, he was definitely getting right down to business. "Yes, that's why I'm taking Dr. Kalaman's extra math course."

"Statistics will be a great help to you," he said, putting his fingertips together, like Nicholas had done in the café. "Why did you decide to go into psychology?"

Bianca hesitated, suddenly wary, then countered with, "Why did you?" There was a pause. She felt uncomfortable and wished, yet again, that she'd thought before blurting something out. It seemed clear by the frown on his face that the psychologist was not impressed.

"More or less by chance," Hasenberg replied finally. "I had started to study medicine—until I realized that even a doctor is nothing more than a psychologist—or a shaman, if you will." The keyboard in the next room chattered quietly, making Bianca feel drowsy. She was still out of breath. The notebook with the cues she had written down for this conversation was in her bag. She had to gain time to gather her thoughts.

"You mean a doctor must also be a good psychologist, and vice versa?"

"It certainly can't hurt," replied Dr. Hasenberg. "But I believe that neither a psychologist nor a doctor can heal the patient. He heals himself. The rituals and symbols are the important thing. No matter whether it's a shaman's mask or a white coat, a spear or a stethoscope—it's trust in the healer's abilities that heals the person. How long have you wanted to be a psychologist?"

"For ever," replied Bianca. The lie slid over her lips with amazing ease. In fact, she had only picked "psychologist" after learning that she would have a better chance of winning a scholarship if she had a definite career goal in mind.

Hasenberg nodded. "Have you done any serious work on it?"

"I've read a few essays—on Jung."

"Good. I would like to give you a list of books today, to work on over the next two weeks. You don't have to memorize them, don't worry, but you should read them carefully and think about them. We'll talk about them at our next meeting."

"And then you'll decide whether you want to be my mentor?"

"We'll both make the decision. Look at this as an opportunity, not a duty. You are interested, aren't you?"

Bianca thought about Tanja's warning and stuck her chin out defiantly. "Of course!"

"Good. Do you have any questions?"

"What's your specialty?"

Dr. Hasenberg leaned back. "Trans-generational research," he said. "Which simply means examining the mechanisms that control a family over generations and exposing their interconnections. Members of a family are often beholden to each other, or mutually dependent, in unseen ways. Because of this, some problems or events occur over and over again. If a grandfather died in an accident, it sometimes happens that there are more accidents in the next generation. That's just a general example, of course."

His voice was pleasant, almost soporific. Bianca's lack of sleep was becoming noticeable. The whole office seemed enveloped in a restful aura as soft as cotton wool. "You might say that we pass on not only our genes but also our tragedies and strokes of fate," he continued. "We remember things for generations, if only subconsciously. You must not interpret the moment: you must look for the pattern."

Bianca suddenly became aware that she had become so tense that her temples were throbbing. She was starting to get a headache. Dr. Hasenberg's words frightened her. She saw her parents before her eyes—and behind them, threatening shadows, phantoms, reaching out for her. Hasenberg's hands were relaxed, holding his glass; he looked almost saintly. His smile seemed to be a mask. When he looked directly at Bianca, however, she thought she saw a flash of annoyance in his eyes. He lifted his glass and drank deeply.

Bianca cleared her throat. "I… I'm more interested in clinical psychology and… psychotropics," she said.

"Ah! The organic approach: accountability, neurotransmitters in the brain, biochemistry—also an interesting subject," he conceded readily. "That's the great thing—every scientific discipline ultimately serves to research the human spirit. If you decide later that you'd rather be a neurologist or biochemist, you can track down engrams, for example."

"Engrams?"

"They're the traces that important events leave in the brain. You can track them and in that way research the way consciousness and memory work."

"Yes… that sounds interesting."

He twisted his mouth into a cool smile.

Bianca thought of Joaquim. "Did you have connections with the Wolves when you were younger?"

He looked at her, bewildered. "What makes you ask that?"

"I'm just interested. I'm writing an essay about the town's history. Earlier you talked about shamans and healers. If you know all about shamanic rituals, you must know some things about the Wolves, too. They have a long tradition, after all."

"I'm afraid I can't help you there. I took part in the procession just once, as a flag-bearer. When I was sixteen or seventeen."

"So you went to the Europa International School?"

"Yes—and I went to the local university, too."

"Do you know what the costumes mean exactly?" Bianca's questions continued. "The masks, the fights—they must all have a symbolic meaning."

"Not a very spectacular one, in psychological terms, " said Dr. Hasenberg, suppressing a yawn. "The wolf is an archaic animal. In many cultures people believe that they are descended from the wolf and connected to his spirit. He's a totem animal. Our wolf's clothing here is probably just a remnant from heathen times, like the Carnival masks in the area you come from."

Dr. Hasenberg smiled faintly, looked at his watch, and stood up. "Good, Bianca. I'll just find that list of the basic literature for you." He searched around in his desk drawer and pulled out a sheet. Bianca could see it was not a short list. Dr. Hasenberg leafed through his appointment calendar. "Two weeks from now, same time?"

"Yes... but... there's something else."

"Do you have another question?"

"What's going on with Joaquim Almán? I don't want to take his place away from him."

Dr. Hasenberg stood up abruptly. "What makes you think that's what's happening?" he returned frostily. In the next room the typing had stopped.

"Isn't Joaquim in your project?"

"Whether and for what reasons other students have terminated their project early is not something you should worry about. Leave those decisions to us. You're not taking anything away from anybody."

Bianca still felt as if she were trying to keep her balance on a swaying tightrope.

Dr. Hasenberg looked at her thoughtfully. Every trace of kindness had left his face. "I'll be honest with you, Bianca. If it were up to me, I would have delayed your mentoring project for at least a year. But Madame Lalonde is convinced that you can organize your time well enough to manage it all. She thinks very highly of you—even though your grades at present are far below expectation." That jab sure hit home. "But I, too, believe," he continued with a civility that sounded forced, "that you have what it takes. Here is your list." He gave her the sheet of paper. "Don't be surprised when you find works on there that relate more to philosophy, or even physics. I like to give my students a global perspective. And there are also books on the list that aren't on the open shelves. Please ask Mr. Nemec to find them for you. He knows where the reserved books are. Try to connect with him today, if you can." Bianca did think it odd that Nemec was in charge of the special collections, but had already started to suspect that he was far more than just the janitor.

IN EXACTLY ONE HOUR the students would head to the dining hall for the evening meal. But right now the hallways were so empty that school seemed no more than a memory. Bianca's steps click-clacked on the linoleum floor. Hasenberg and Nemec, she repeated mentally. What do they have to do with each other? She ran down the stairs, turning toward the language labs. She had never noticed that slight echo before. She could hear her steps just a split second later. It sounded as if someone was running after her. Bianca stopped. Now it was dead silent again. Quietly she went on. The echo was still there. And there was something else—a click, but not of heels. Abruptly she stood still again and listened. Directly behind her someone took another step. Bianca gripped her pen like a weapon and swung around. The hallway was empty; she could hear nothing but her own breath. Carefully she took a step back, then another. There—someone or something was sniffing the air, as if it was trying to find Bianca's scent, and then there were three clicks, one after the other. A presence surrounded her, so close it felt like someone was standing directly in front of her. She imagined that a breath brushed her hand, and she screamed. The sniffing stopped and Bianca was there alone, feeling as though an icy wind had taken hold of her.

"DID HE TEAR YOU TO SHREDS?" asked Caitlin. She was lying on her bed in the middle of an avalanche of books. The day after tomorrow she would write the first of her final exams, and even Caitlin, always so relaxed, was pale at the thought and had no appetite.

"Hardly," replied Bianca, throwing herself into Caitlin's reading chair. She was still freezing, and when she rubbed her lower arms she felt goose bumps.

"And?" her friend persisted, without looking up from her books.

"He gave me a list of books I need to get from the library."

"Oh, then they're sure to be special books that you can only get from Igor."

"Igor?"

"Nemec—doesn't he remind you of Frankenstein's servant?"

Gradually Bianca was finding her way back to reality. That presence—it must have been a draft, she told herself, just her imagination playing tricks.

"Let's see!" said Caitlin, stretching out her hand for the list. Bianca hesitated a moment too long. Caitlin wrinkled her brow and let her hand fall.

"Enough, already!" she cried. Her green eyes flashed. She jumped up from the bed and moved toward Bianca. "How many times do I have to tell you I'm sorry? I didn't mean to rat you out. I'll never talk to you about your nightmares again, though I worry, and you talk in your sleep. And I'll be a good girl and lock my door so you'll feel safer. But it doesn't matter what I do—you don't trust anyone, do you?" On edge, she ran her fingers through her hair and sighed. "Sorry," she said softly. "I didn't mean to attack you. It's just... I'm really wound up because of the exam. And I'm not very good at handling this strange atmosphere between us."

Bianca had never seen Caitlin in such low spirits. Nicholas's words came into her head, and she felt ashamed of her distrust. "Sorry, Caitlin. No more bad moods."

Caitlin visibly relaxed and smiled hesitantly at Bianca. She was just about to say something else when her cell phone rang. Bianca went into her own room. She lay down on the bed and closed her eyes. She could hear Caitlin's muffled conversation through the door. She couldn't really hear much, but it didn't sound like she was talking to a member of her family. A few minutes later Caitlin stuck her curly head through the door. Bianca had never been so relieved to see a smile.

"I'm meeting Jan in the library café," said Caitlin. "Do you want to come with me?

TODAY ALL THE READING TABLES were occupied. With a dull feeling in the pit of her stomach, Bianca looked around for the Wolves, but could not see any of them. She could look down into the café area through the glass facade behind the bookcase containing the dictionaries. Caitlin was sitting with Jan at a table, beaming. The pair obviously had a lot to talk about. Bianca watched them for a while, then plucked up her courage and went to look for Simon "Igor" Nemec. Her secret hope that he was not there was not to be. She had scarcely left the languages section when he approached her. A sharp peppermint smell wafted toward Bianca. However, Igor's eyes were not red today.

"Dr. Hasenberg's list?" he growled, before she had said anything.

She nodded and held it out to him.

He glanced at it. "Don't need it," he said, waving it off, and indicating that she should follow him. She did, and noticed that the way he held his stiff shoulders made him look as if he was trying to hold his ears shut with them. He led her past the psychology section; they passed physics, metaphysics, and biology, came to the history section, and finally reached a corner of the older part of the library, the same area Nemec had chased Bianca out of at their last meeting. Nemec stopped and started taking books from the shelves. He seemed to be following a well-practiced choreography. How many students' hands had these volumes passed through before hers?

Nemec piled the books up and set them down on a shelf near the psychology section. Then he grasped a broad wall of shelves and simply swung it aside. Bianca's mouth hung open. So! There *was* a door behind the shelves—she had just been looking in the wrong corner when Nemec had caught her. The door was hardly visible, mind you, as it was wallpapered the same as the wall. Nemec pulled out his key ring. His fingers trembling slightly, he picked out a flat key and opened the door. Behind it yawned a black hole. A weak odor of leather and dust reached Bianca's nostrils. A hideous fluorescent light blinked on, flickering. Nemec stepped into the room and let go of the door handle. With a harsh creak that became a whine, the door closed behind him. Bianca grabbed the nearest bookshelf and held on to it tightly. Like a flash photo, Bianca suddenly saw herself in the foyer of the library a moment before finding the woman's body. There was just darkness—and a sound. This sound. A moment later Nemec came back out of the little room.

"Here," he said, heaving the whole pile of books into her arms. The bandage on his right hand did not look so new any more. At the sight of his sinewy hands Bianca imagined these hands killing Annette Durlain. Don't flip out, she warned herself. The noise just meant that someone else as well as Annette Durlain must have been in the library. Nemec—or someone else.

"Have you been doing the museum tours for long?" she asked.

Nemec's eyes were watery and yellowish. To her surprise he smiled at her fleetingly. "A quarter-century," he answered. "And it doesn't get any more exciting as the years go by."

"Do you still remember some of the visitors?"

"You mean Annette Durlain, don't you? No, kiddo. Do you think I notice every face?"

He sighed deeply and suddenly looked like nothing more than a pitiable old man who had somewhere, somehow, lost his grip on life.

"So you didn't know her?"

He shook his head wearily.

"So why are you so sad?"

"Life is sometimes enough to make you weep, don't you think?"

Bianca lowered her gaze and looked at the topmost book. On the cover was a stamped picture: a lion who had bitten into a sun.

"Is... this book really on the list?" she asked in a weak voice.

"Of course."

"What's it about?"

"The lion who ate the sun," he said. "The magic symbol for the philosopher's stone. It's a book about Faust, who practiced the black arts, and his experiments in alchemy."

THE LOAD OF BOOKS pressed heavily on Bianca's hips as she ran down the stairs to the exit. The evening sun had laid a golden veil over the grass and bathed the manor house in an insubstantial light that nevertheless emphasized its sharp contours. With quick steps Bianca ran along the wall for a little way, to a place where there was nothing but ivy and stonework. Here she took time to catch her breath. Her fear of the Wolves, which made her anxious and irritable inside the school building, disappeared out here as if by magic. Relieved, she took out her cell phone.

"Nicholas, it's me!"

"Why are you speaking so softly? Where are you?"

"Behind the manor house—I needed some air."

"I was going to call you in a second, anyway. The museum lady got suspicious and won't give me the Feverlin address. I spent nearly the whole evening in the Internet café, but the Feverlins I found there don't seem to be the ones we're looking for. Tomorrow I'll get on the phone again."

"You can save yourself the trouble. " She lowered her voice to a whisper. "I know where Annette Durlain was searching. I'm sure now that she wasn't alone in the library! And if I'm right, we may well find the chronicles that are not supposed to exist."

"Where?"

"In a special little room off the library. I just don't know how to get in yet. The room is locked and I don't think it has a window."

"Got it," said Nicholas. "Time for Plan B."

SHADOWS

CAITLIN WAS TOO NERVOUS to drink her morning tea. Her pencil case fell out of her hand for the third time, as she checked to see if she had all her pens and pencils, and whether they all worked or were sharp.

"What's the first subject?" asked Bianca.

Caitlin rolled her eyes. "History—two hours. Then a break. Then oral exams in French and Spanish. And then this afternoon, physics."

"I'm sure you'll write the best exam ever and get into Trinity College Dublin with flying colors. You can do it!"

"If I write the exam the way I feel, I'll be back home in Dingle in a week, applying for a job washing up at O'Reilly's. Thanks all the same!" Caitlin hugged Bianca in a brief goodbye and grabbed her bag. The next moment she was gone. Bianca heard voices in the hallway and fast steps disappearing into the distance. The morning's tensions fell away, and her weariness returned. She rubbed her eyes and crept back into bed. She still had ten minutes before she had to leave—and while she was listening to Mrs. Lincoln's explanations about new aspects of English grammar, Caitlin would be sweating over her exam paper like the sixteen other examinees. Other duties awaited Bianca, however. Above all she had to get used to the idea that tonight she would be risking her future at the Europa International School. She must be crazy. Nervously she looked at her alarm clock and checked her calculations. Seventeen more hours until she would meet Nicholas. The timing was perfect. With all the teachers and students concentrating on exams, they could not have hoped for a better distraction. She closed her eyes and imagined the route she would take tonight.

None of the Wolves appeared the whole day. That surprised Bianca at first, but then it occurred to her that some students must have been assigned the task of making sure the exam area remained quiet. At her reading table in the library, Bianca tried without success to concentrate on her homework. Today the formulas and diagrams looked like cryptic signs, whose meanings she could scarcely remember. The lack of sleep and the dreams worried her. *I just have to hold on for one more day,* she told herself. The answers were almost within her reach. A haggard-looking Caitlin rushed by on the floor below. She was following five other students, who looked just as tense. As if aware of Bianca's gaze, Caitlin looked up. She beamed and gave a thumbs-up.

THE MINUTES WERE CREEPING BY, more slowly than Bianca thought possible. For an hour she had done nothing but stare at her cell phone and the clock. Luckily Caitlin had been so exhausted that despite her nervousness about the next day's exams she had gone to sleep quickly. Finally the numbers changed. One o'clock. Quietly Bianca got up and slid the phone into a pocket of her sweatpants. Without making a sound, she opened the door and slipped into the hallway. Because she had spent the last hour in darkness, her eyes had adjusted to the gloom; she could make out the doors to the other rooms and the glass door at the end of the corridor. Somewhere a toilet flushed; light shone through the crack under a door. Bianca hurried on, leaving the girls' quarters, and fumbled her way down the stairs. The alcove under the main staircase was dark. Bianca stopped at the place they had agreed on and peered into the shadows.

"Nicholas?" she whispered. A scraping noise answered her. Heart pounding, she stood still, her right shoulder pressed against the cool stone of the staircase. Then she heard someone clearing his throat quietly. Bianca was so relieved that her legs nearly buckled. "Nicholas!" With clammy fingers she felt for the tiny flashlight that she had taken off her key chain.

"Nope," said a voice. Bianca jumped back; the flashlight slipped out of her fingers and hit the floor. "If you stand there, anyone in the park can see you through the glass. Come with me!"

"Jan?"

A shadow rushed past, beckoning to her. Bianca felt for her flashlight. Something clicked in the darkness, then she heard a snap that sounded like something electric turning on. A badly oiled door hinge creaked softly.

"Come on!" hissed the voice. With knees of jelly Bianca started to move. The door to the map room, usually locked, was open. The next moment a flashlight switched on. A cone of light moved quickly over rolled-up maps and battered card-board boxes. Bianca blinked. Jan too was wearing a long T-shirt and sweatpants that bagged around his legs.

"In or out!" he said.

She gulped and went into the room. The door shut with a snap. Jan put the flashlight on a shelf and set a bag down on the floor. It rattled.

"What are you doing here?" whispered Bianca. He laughed, half asleep, and rummaged in the bag. Bianca looked at his tousled hair. The crumpled T-shirt he was wearing was probably his pajama top. He took something out of the bag that looked like an electric toothbrush without its brush attachment.

"I see," said Bianca sarcastically. "You're planning to move in here."

Just then her cell phone vibrated. In trying to take it out as quickly as possible, she almost dropped it.

"Is he there?" whispered Nicholas's voice.

"You sent him here?"

She heard his sigh of relief. "Thank God! Then it's working out all right—listen, I can't get away. But Jan knows what to do."

"You're not serious! God damn it, couldn't you have told me before?"

Jan laid a warning finger on his lips.

"Sorry," whispered Nicholas, genuinely contrite. "I swear there's a good reason. I'll explain later."

"Fine. Then have a nice evening!" snapped Bianca, pressing the "Off" button on her phone. The display went blank.

"Well, I guess dear Nick gave us both a surprise," said Jan, yawning. Again he bent down and rummaged in his bag. "What sort of a key did Nemec use?" he asked.

"Why do you want to know?"

Jan held up the toothbrush. "Universal key," he said quietly. "But I have to know what attachment I need."

"The toothbrush is a key?"

Jan nodded. "Door opener. Of course I beefed it up, otherwise the rpm would be too slow. You can use it to brush your teeth, too, of course," he added ironically.

"Flat key," said Bianca. "About as long as my little flashlight here, with lengthwise grooves."

"Standard security lock," said Jan, shaking his head, "So, basically, just as secure as the other doors in this building." Fascinated despite herself, Bianca watched him select a metal attachment and slide the remaining steel pins into the pockets of his baggy pants.

"You really built that yourself?"

"Sure—I also built the radio control for your kettle, remember?"

"I thought you were an artist."

"What do you think I do in the art room—just mess about with clay? First of all, the art room is further away from the bedrooms and the janitor's apartment than any other so no one can hear me—and second, there's a high-powered kiln there."

Bianca shivered. "And your toothbrush works on a security lock?"

"Sure—you just stick this attachment into the keyhole and turn it on. The vibration turns the steel barrel and—click! The door's open."

"Why build something like that?"

Jan shrugged and pushed his bag under a shelf. "I have a thing about locked doors."

In the light of the flashlight he actually looked nineteen for once. For the first time she realized how strong he was.

"You missed two years of school. Were you... sick or something?"

"Reform school. One year for grand larceny. I lost the other year because I failed." He smiled sweetly. "Hey, cat got your tongue?"

"No... I..."

"Ah, you didn't expect to hear that kind of story at this venerable school? Never heard of the quota?"

"The scholarships for disadvantaged students?"

Jan laughed softly. "No one would ever put it that way, of course—sounds too much like discrimination. If you look at it like that, Madame bought my freedom, yes. I was surprised myself that I was so good at physics. It was a chance to get away from my stepfather. But, of course, here I have special conditions. All the parents had to sign a form saying they agree I can be here." He smiled ironically. "Yours, too."

Bianca was flabbergasted. "And Caitlin? Does she know?"

"Sure," he replied shortly, adding rather crossly: "At least she didn't make as big a deal of it as you."

"Why did you..."

Jan rolled his eyes and raised his arms dramatically. "Oh, God, not that question again," he whispered. "Why? Why? Because... nothing's easier than breaking into cars. Because it brought in money, because the weather was good. No idea. Because I'm a loser? You tell me—it's your specialty, isn't it, explaining to people what makes them tick."

"I can't be much of a psychologist. I thought you were just a coward."

"Oh, you're not far wrong there," he replied calmly. "I am pretty cowardly. But a door is only a door." Nervously he tugged at his T-shirt and looked at Bianca pleadingly.

"You won't tell Cait anything about this little outing?"

"I promise," replied Bianca. "As long as you don't tell her either!"

"Let's shake on it!" They shook. "Let's go, we need to hurry."

"Wait a minute," she whispered, gripping Jan's arm to hold him back as he reached for the door handle.

"Nicholas and you—how do you know each other?"

"Nicholas is a really good guy. Medical student with money. We really just know each other by sight. His motorbike is a heap of rust. I soldered a few connections for him and gave him some information—about you, too."

"So you were the one who told him about the book about saints," Bianca said. "What's he paying for tonight's action?"

Jan clicked his tongue and shook his head. "That's classified information! But the book you want seems to be important."

IT FELT SPOOKY, walking at night in the hallways that she knew only from the daytime. Jan went ahead with such a sure step that it seemed he could see in the dark. He often had to stop and wait until Bianca had felt her way along the walls to him. He led her to the library via back stairs that Bianca had never seen. With a click, the door opened under Jan's expert hands and they entered the library from a side wing. Moonlight shone through the blinds and threw a net of pale threads of light over the reading tables and shelves.

"Which section is the door in?" whispered Jan. Bianca got her bearings in the gloom, recognizing the crooked bookshelves containing the dictionaries, and felt her way further. Finally the wall with the door gleamed ahead of her. With their combined strength they pushed the bookshelf aside. Jan kneeled in front of the lock. For a moment the light of his flashlight flashed on, then went out immediately. There was a click, then a fast vibration, which seemed to Bianca as loud as a circular saw. Frightened, she looked round, but nothing was moving. With a dragging noise the door opened inwards. Quickly they slipped into the room and closed the door behind them carefully so it would not creak. Immediately the fluorescent light came on. Jan took his hand off the light switch.

"There's no danger—there are no windows," he whispered, smiling at Bianca's horrified face. His eyes were gleaming. He looked around the little room eagerly. If Bianca had wondered before what could make Jan risk losing his chance to prove himself, it was clear to her now that he lived for moments like this: for control, secrecy, the feeling of simply being able to go where no door could block his way.

"That's a lot of books," he said. "I hope you know what you're looking for."

The room was bigger than it seemed at first glance. What made it look so small were the deep bookshelves, in which two rows of books stood one behind the other. Right at the back sat an ancient copy machine. Bianca could not make out any logical order. The place looked like the brain of a crazy scientist who could not distinguish between what was important and what was not. A few book spines were decorated with gold writing; others had been new a decade ago but had now taken on a brownish-yellow tinge. Bianca's gaze fell on a row of yellowed chronicles and yearbooks. On each book cover the year was given: the first said "1649–1700." On the next book it was "1701–1750," continuing in the same way up to the year 2000.

An hour later Bianca was close to despair. She was finding only statistics about the locality, lists of houses, the accounts of various associations and trusts, the dealings of the volunteer fire brigade, and whole bundles of copper engravings. No sign of the convent's history—and no sign of the Wolves. Tirelessly she searched row after row. Again and again Jan had to suppress a sneeze as a cloud of dust went up his nose. They were extra careful to put the books back exactly where they had come from, matching them up with the marks left in the dust. Finally, when they got to the medical reference works, Bianca put her hand on a thin, worn booklet with a binding of firm cardboard. Carefully she pulled it out. The edges were already curling and the book was coming apart. Bianca laid it on the floor gently, kneeled before it, and began to leaf through it page by page.

"Here's something!" she whispered. It was a Wolves' club record book—only three years old, but better than nothing. When she started reading through it, however, she was disappointed. All the expenses for new costumes were listed in excruciating detail, and bills from a Carnival store were stapled to the edge. Then there was a training schedule and choreography for the stick dance. The last entries were the members' names and contacts at the local Carnival Association.

"Crap," she murmured. "That can't be right." Again she looked through it page by page, but there was nothing to help her. Here and there someone had scribbled something in the margin—had maybe been chatting on the phone and doodling on the booklet. One of these artists had tried to draw a human figure. Bianca leaned closer over the booklet.

"Jan," she whispered, "What do you think this is?"

He kneeled down beside her and looked at the drawing.

"Boobs," he said. "Someone must have been drawing his girlfriend."

"And below it—what's that?" Bianca pointed to a symbol that had been partially crossed out.

"Hmm. His girlfriend must have had a tattoo. Do you need the picture?" Bianca nodded. "Better get the names, too. Do you have a digital camera with you?"

"No."

"Shit," said Jan, just like Caitlin when she was having a bad day. "Nicholas was going to bring the camera. But wait a minute—we don't need one!"

He jumped up and plugged in the copy machine. Humming, it began to warm up. Bianca got to her feet and looked nervously at the door.

"Somebody might hear that!" she whispered. Jan waved the idea aside.

"Don't worry. It won't take long."

"And the counter? What if someone notices that the counter has moved?"

Jan half smiled. "Abracadabra," he said, taking out a match. "It's an ancient machine. It has a mechanical counter, no digital stuff. All I have to do is interrupt the meter pulse."

Bianca watched uneasily as Jan opened the front panel of the copy machine, removed a metal coupling from the counter mechanism, and jammed the match into position. After copying the booklet unhurriedly, he took the match out again and draped the cable exactly the way it had been before. Bianca took the small pile of pages and quickly stuffed it under her T-shirt.

When they turned the light out again, they were both completely blind. Their fingers met by chance in the darkness, and without a word they held hands as they felt their way forward together. Moonlight gleamed on the metal arms of the reading lamps, and gradually the tables and chairs emerged from the darkness. The shelves towered in the aisles like stone giants. Metaphysics, physics, chemistry: Bianca counted them off mentally. Together they slipped between the shelves into a side passage. There they had to separate so they could walk in single file.

"Wait, Jan!" she whispered.

He stopped and turned around. "What?"

"I'm going back to my room via the main stairs. It's... shorter."

A shadowy shrug. "Fine," he replied quietly. "I'm going out the back way again. See you!"

He ducked down and disappeared into the darkness. Bianca waited until his stealthy steps faded into the distance. Then, legs like jelly, she followed Annette Durlain's trail. Had she found what she wanted in the room? Had she taken it, carrying it with her on the way to the stairs? Bianca took a deep breath and crept around the shelves. She took four, five steps toward the main stairs, then froze. The sound of a step behind her stopped instantly. Bianca hesitated, then turned around. Since when had there been a chair in this aisle? Straining, she tried to see more clearly. No doubt about it, the chair... was standing up! The chair legs left the floor and the whole thing became a swaying shadow as tall as a man. Nemec? Bianca heard a scraping sound, then the phantom moved. Strange breath flowed through the gaps in the bookshelves like smoke. Over the top of a row of book spines Bianca could see the figure turning around, and a shadowy head turned toward her. Her body reacted instinctively. She rushed toward the door. Too late she realized that the figure that jumped out at her the next moment was her own image in the glass door. Without knowing how she got there, she found herself between two rows of bookshelves again. Her muscles hurt. Book spines dug into her shoulder blades. Then something hit her head. Her knees gave way, then everything went black.

HAD IT BEEN ONE of her bad dreams? Dental enamel shone in the moonlight. Warm saliva was dripping onto her hand. A stinging pain pierced her scalp. She struggled to open her eyes and felt for her bedside lamp. But all she found was the metal foot of a bookshelf. In the darkness she opened her eyes and saw the pale eyes of the phantom staring at her. The next moment it was on her. A hand lay on her mouth and stifled her cry. A ray of light appeared from nowhere. Dazed, she blinked and did not try to defend herself when someone laid a hand on her forehead. It even felt good, because the pain lessened. "You're dreaming," murmured a voice, and she sank back, relieved.

The next thing she was aware of was the library's scratchy carpet against her cheek and the moonlight still shining in between the slats of the blinds. Dazed, she looked around and a wave of shock hit her. What she had taken for dripping saliva was her own blood—at the hairline her scalp was throbbing, and when she carefully felt the spot, she felt a small cut, which was already forming a scab. Presumably responsible was the book that had fallen on her head and now lay on the floor, a little off to the side: *Shakespeare's Collected Works, Volume IV.* She must have bumped into the shelf, and the book had fallen down and hit her head. The cut on her temple was from the corner of its hard cover. She touched her T-shirt and heaved a sigh of relief. The copies were still there!

She had to struggle to get to her feet and put the heavy book back on the shelf. Then she headed for the stairs, legs shaking, expecting at any moment to hear a voice behind her ordering her to stop.

MAYBE IT WAS BECAUSE she was still dazed: when she entered her room, she stumbled over the chair that she had placed beside the adjoining door earlier. Before she was back on her feet, she heard Caitlin's sleepy voice. "Bianca?" Light appeared under the door, and the next moment the door swung open.

When Caitlin saw Bianca, she opened her eyes wide. "Oh my God!"

"Shh!" said Bianca. "Calm down! Everything's OK."

"Everything's OK? You're bleeding! Where've you been? Who did this?" Then Caitlin suddenly put her hand to her mouth. "Did… Joaquim do that?"

"No," Bianca said, exasperated. "No one did anything to me—I tripped."

Someone banged on the wall.

Caitlin lowered her voice. "You tripped in the middle of the night? Don't bullshit me, Bianca—you have shoes on, and you don't sleep in your sweatpants! What did they do to you?"

"No one did anything to me!"

Caitlin surveyed the cut, and the strands of hair all stuck together. "That's enough," she said. "We're going to Madame, right now! Something's going on, and it's clear that you can't deal with it alone."

"No way!" Bianca grasped Caitlin's wrists. "Listen to me. If we report this, I'll be thrown out. The only thing that will help me now is an alibi. I can't tell you what happened, but it's possible that Nemec will knock at my door in a few minutes, and then—please!—tell him you don't think I've been out of the room." Beseechingly she went on: "Something big is going on, but I can't tell you everything. I'll go to Madame as soon as I have more proof. Please just trust me."

Caitlin broke free and stepped back. Thoughtfully, she rubbed her wrists and looked at Bianca.

"Proof?" she asked suspiciously. "Of what?"

"I can't say."

"I'm your friend!"

"Are you?" The words slipped out. Instantly she regretted it. Caitlin looked as if Bianca had slapped her.

"You still don't trust me," she said. "What do you think I am? Do you really think I want to make you look bad to Madame Lalonde? God, there are better ways I could've done that! What would be the point? I just want to finish school here and go back to Ireland. Nothing else."

Bianca's silence made Caitlin angrier.

"You can't imagine anyone simply liking you, can you?" she hissed. "What do I have to do to make you trust me? Some sort of proof?"

Bianca raised her head and looked Caitlin in the eye. "Your T-shirt," she said, gesturing toward Caitlin's hip. "Pull it up."

Caitlin stared at her as if she had finally lost her mind, then she crossed her arms, took hold of the hem, and pulled the T-shirt over her head. Angrily she flung the shirt on Bianca's bed. She stood there, in just her underwear. Her skin was flawless.

"So?" she asked, stretching her arms out to the sides. "What are you looking for?"

Bianca picked up the T-shirt and gave it to Caitlin. She felt foolish. Yet at the same time she was extremely relieved.

"I thought you might have a tattoo," she said apologetically.

"I see," said Caitlin sarcastically. "Well, I don't. So now are you going to tell me what happened to you?"

Bianca considered how much she should tell her. Finally she pulled out the copies with the names. Quickly she told her about the threats by the Wolves and about Nicholas, who was having the same problems she was. She did not tell her about the forged autopsy report or her meeting with Jan.

"And tonight I was in Nemec's book room, to find out more about the Wolves. But there was someone in the library—I think Nemec saw me. Maybe he's reporting it right now. If he is, tomorrow I can pack my bags and go home."

Caitlin's eyes had narrowed to slits. "So you broke in—into a room that has a security lock?"

Bianca held her breath.

Caitlin suddenly looked as if she'd bitten into a lemon. "Shit!" she said. Without looking at her friend, she went into her room and slammed the door behind her. A few seconds later Bianca heard her on the phone. She was whispering, but still, Bianca was glad she was not in Jan's place.

MADDALINA

BIANCA LAY IN BED in the dark, expecting to hear a knock at her door at any minute. The cut, which she had doctored herself as well as she could, had formed a scab, but it still throbbed with every beat of her heart. Six o'clock passed, then seven, and nothing happened—and finally, at quarter past seven, Caitlin headed out to her next exam marathon, her eyes puffy. Bianca switched her cell phone back on. Eleven missed calls from Nicholas. Just as she was about to call him back, the phone rang in her hand.

"Thank God!" cried Nicholas. "Did everything go according to plan? Why didn't you call?"

"Because I'm lying in bed with a cut on my head, and today they're going to throw me out—I'm not sure, but I think Nemec saw me."

"A cut? Are you OK?"

Although she was furious with him, it was good to hear him worrying more about her than about Nemec.

"Someone knocked me down."

"Who?"

"Shakespeare."

Nicholas hesitated for a moment. "Your first class doesn't start for twenty minutes. Let's meet!"

"No!" she cried, and then immediately lowered her voice. "No, I'm fine, a book just fell on my head. I hope your excuse is just as original."

"Look out of the window," he answered dryly.

Bianca got up, ignoring the slight dizziness that hit her as she did so, and gripped her cell phone between her shoulder and her ear. It was hard work pulling the blinds up in this contorted position. Morning sunlight bathed her face. She blinked and looked towards the parking lot. She would have recognized those hunched shoulders anywhere. When he saw her waving to him, a relieved smile spread across his face. "Well, at least you can still stand," he said. "And now look at what happened to me last night."

There was a rustling sound as he put the cell phone in his pocket, bent down, and rolled up his right pants leg. A bandage came into view. His entire shin looked like an abstract painting in a wide variety of red and blue tones. Nicholas put his cell phone to his ear again. "Damn road," he said, shrugging. "On the right-hand curve near the last traffic light. I was on my way here. A car stopped and took me to emergency."

"Welcome to the club," replied Bianca dryly.

"Luckily the bike still runs," he said. "What do you think, when can we meet?"

"I don't know. I… I'm wondering whether I should go to Madame."

He stared up at the window in silence. Bianca heard his breath at her ear.

"We have next to no proof," he reminded her. "And what if your policeman really is involved in all this?"

"I know," Bianca replied sharply. In the pause that followed, she noticed him nervously lighting a cigarette.

"You choose," he said finally. "Tell the office, and we're busted. Then we probably both lose our place in this town. Or we finish this."

They looked into each other's eyes across the distance.

"Anyway, there is one piece of good news," he said quietly. "I, alias Jehle, have an appointment tomorrow with a lady whose dead husband's grandfather was called Heinrich Feverlin."

REALLY, NOTHING COULD GO WRONG. The three of them left the school after breakfast on Saturday and crossed the parking lot. It was a hive of activity. Car doors opened, and parents got out with big bags and packages, handing their sons and daughters the promised jacket, books, or pile of CDs. The air shimmered with family, but today Bianca had no time to let it ruin her mood. She was keeping an eye open for Simon Nemec. He had not been in the library, and no one had spoken to her all day. No teacher had summoned her with a serious expression to the office. It was spooky.

"Stop tugging at your hair," whispered Caitlin to her. Bianca only now noticed that she was playing with the strand that she had combed over the scab and bruise. Jan walked beside Caitlin in silence, like a dog that had been whipped. The tension between the two of them was so tangible that the air around them seemed charged with electricity. At least Caitlin's exam had gone very well. In the evening she had checked and figured out that she had answered eight of the ten questions correctly. Now she felt confident—and furious with Jan. The day would be anything but a romantic outing for him. Three abreast, they crossed the parking lot in silence and headed toward the bus stop. As always when she left the school, Bianca felt a heavy weight lift from her shoulders. Rounding the corner, heading toward the gate, she nearly bumped into Madame Lalonde.

"Oops!" said Madame. She was wearing a dark-green suit that emphasized the color of her eyes, and she had a small suitcase in her hand. When she saw Bianca, a smile flitted across her face. "Oh, Bianca—good morning!"

"Good morning," answered Bianca and Jan in unison.

"I'm glad I met you. I saw on the schedule that once again you're not going to see your parents?"

Bianca nodded and suppressed the urge to smooth her hair.

"We're going to the pool," Caitlin said in turn.

Marie-Claire raised her eyebrows. "Too bad. If I'd known sooner that you had plans... I'm going to Brussels until Wednesday, but I've asked Dr. Hasenberg to speak to you. There's a lunch here today. A few of the other psychologists from the university will be there, too. I thought you might be interested in joining them."

Bianca had the feeling that the headmistress knew everything. Her swimming bag lay in her hand like a lie as heavy as lead. And the fact that Madame was leaving her here with the Wolves and Simon Nemec made her even more uneasy. Caitlin hooked her arm through hers.

"Thank you for the offer," said Bianca finally. "But I haven't even started to read the books on the list Dr. Hasenberg gave me."

Madame Lalonde laughed. Bianca realized that she looked tired and had dark circles under her eyes.

"Whatever you think. You're right—we stuff you full of

enough knowledge as it is—Caitlin can tell you all about that, can't you, Caitlin?"

Caitlin smiled a little too nicely. A taxi door banged. The driver got out and opened the trunk, and Madame dropped in her case. She waved goodbye and got into the taxi.

"What's she doing in Brussels?" whispered Bianca to Caitlin.

"As far as I know, she's giving a presentation on the concept of the school and looking for more backers," replied Caitlin.

Jan looked at the taxi as it drove away, interested.

"Well, you seem to be well in with Madame Lalonde," he said.

So far, thought Bianca gloomily.

NICHOLAS WAS WAITING at the bus stop as arranged, a motorbike helmet in each hand.

"So that's him," murmured Caitlin to her. "Now I get it!"

Bianca was annoyed to realize she was blushing. "Thanks for the alibi,' she said briskly. "I'll be back by five."

"We're late," grumbled Nicholas, passing her the helmet. "Let's see—is that where you got hurt?"

She nodded silently and let Nicholas move closer to brush her hair off her forehead.

"Ouch," he said. "That was a big book. Do you think you can get the helmet on?"

"Sure!" He looked at her for a moment that seemed to last forever, and then smiled at her. She took the helmet and carefully put it on, while Nicholas got onto the bike. It took him a while to manipulate his injured leg and settle into his seat.

It was a strange feeling, climbing on behind Nicholas. Without asking he took her hands and pulled them towards him, until she was holding him above his hips. The motorbike lurched just once, then the centrifugal force pulled her backward, and they roared along the main road, heading out of town toward the west.

The trip took more than an hour. It was nearly 40 miles on the highway to the next large town, and then the route continued through several villages. Each was smaller than the one before. The roads got worse, too, until finally Nicholas and Bianca were driving on something only slightly better than a cart track. A sign saying "Kosrow" was rammed deep into the ground.

"It's number four, High Street," Nicholas said, once he had taken off his helmet and shaken his hair, which was soaked with sweat. They looked around and saw a white house.

THE WOMAN WHO OPENED THE DOOR to them did not look at all like a grieving widow. She had a deep frown line between her eyes, and curly hair, dyed blue-black. Bianca guessed she was fifty. She wore dark red lipstick that matched her red and black blouse. Nicholas smiled at her winningly.

"Good afternoon, Mrs. Meyer," he said, holding out his press card. "Klaus Jehle. We phoned you. This is Martina Huber, who's doing an internship with us."

The woman's face lit up immediately. "How nice. Do come in." Her soft voice was unexpected in view of her severe appearance.

They followed Mrs. Meyer through a long, narrow hallway that was painted a discreet blue. Color photos looked down accusingly on the intruders. There was a peculiar smell coming from the living room. As soon as Bianca entered the small room, she realized its source: on the walls hung dozens of stuffed animal heads and birds. She could see deer, goat, the head of a wild boar, and several pheasants. African masks made of wood had been hung between them. A strange contrast to the modern leather-upholstered furniture and glass cases.

"Would you like some orange juice?" asked Mrs. Meyer. Nicholas thanked her and nodded, and her exit to the kitchen gave them time to survey the room at their leisure.

"Oh, you found the masks," said Mrs. Meyer, coming back into the room with a tray. "Yes, my grandfather-in-law, if you can say that, traveled a lot—he was a sailor and lived in Africa for a long time. My husband..." the short pause was almost imperceptible "...inherited his estate about twenty years ago." She smiled and put the tray down on the glass table in front of the sofa. "Help yourselves! Are you both students at the university?"

Bianca shook her head. "I'm still at school, but I want to be a journalist."

"Oh—what school do you go to?"

"Lessing High School in Ammring," Nicholas answered for her.

"I don't know that one. My stepson from my husband's first marriage used to go to the Europa International School. It's not far from the university. An excellent school—you should try to get in there, Martina."

Bianca cleared her throat. "I thought about it. Maybe I'll apply next year."

"Do that. It's a once-in-a-lifetime opportunity. My stepson went straight from there to London, where he studied Business Administration. Mr. Sanger, the headmaster at that time, really did a lot for us. As a thank you, my husband gave the Maddalina of Trenta Foundation some of the original documents from the estate."

Nicholas and Bianca exchanged a quick glance.

"What exactly are you taking at university?" Mrs. Meyer turned to Nicholas.

"History," he replied promptly. "At the moment I'm looking at the history of the town in the seventeenth century. That means I'm working on part of your family history."

"My husband's family history," Mrs. Meyer corrected him seriously. "Well, as I told you over the phone, I'm not sure whether my documents will be any help. It might make more sense for you to ask the Foundation directly. But I'll be happy to show you the documents that I could find, anyway. You've already seen the executioner's sword and the hangman's certificate, of course."

"I'm sure you can help us," said Nicholas, beaming at her. "Thanks so much for going to so much trouble!"

Mrs. Meyer smiled. "I was tidying up, anyway. The house is going to be sold soon. I've brought out everything I could find from that time, but there's not much: just a few documents and photos. My husband and I never bothered about the papers. Oh well, see for yourself whether you can use them." With these words she got up and went into the hallway. They could hear a drawer opening in the next room.

"So, once again no original documents," whispered Nicholas. Impatience made him sound curt. The masks and glass animal eyes seemed to stare at them as they waited. Finally Mrs. Meyer came back into the room, carrying a stack of envelopes and papers in plastic covers. Right on top lay a worn notebook.

"Here," she said, laying the bundle on the coffee table. "These have been in the attic for more than twenty years. My husband just couldn't throw anything away. Take a look at them, and if you need anything or have any questions, call me—I'll be next door in my study."

They thanked her and waited until she had left the room. Then they dove into the papers. The dust made Bianca's nose itch; it stank of mice and old wood. Mrs. Meyer was right—there was not much there. There were a few ancient banknotes and with them several documents regarding the purchase of farmland in the nineteenth century. In one envelope there were numbered photos showing various town buildings around the turn of the century. Bianca recognized the facade of the university, the old town hall, several streets in the old town, and finally the manor house. Impatiently they worked their way through the more recent documents. Copies of passports turned up between older papers. Finally Bianca reached for the notebook. "Heinrich Feverlin" was written on the first page. "That must have been Mr. Meyer's grandfather."

The paper was so dry that it felt like it would crumble into dust at the first touch. Every page was closely written in a cramped hand but was nevertheless legible. Obviously Mr. Feverlin had used the notebook for his household accounts, to record his monthly income and expenses. More than thirty pages contained only accounts. Bianca leafed through further and gave a start.

"Nicholas! Here's something!"

He came so close to her that his hair brushed her cheek.

"He copied the hangman's records before he gave them to the school. The original records!"

Johann Georg Feverlin had been an honest man, and God-fearing too. On every page he praised God so many times that after three pages Heinrich Feverlin had started to use just abbreviations to note them. Maybe his belief in God was all the executioner could cling on to in 1651—after the Belverinas' trial. Putting heart and soul into it, he had recorded one interrogation after another, every disturbing detail. In his version Maddalina and her nuns were not the kind of witches who called up thunder and hail. They called up something much worse.

Nicholas brought out a digital camera.

Thus did Bernhard Haussman Kohlbauer Swear before the Exorcist that on April 24th Evening He was on the Way to his Field, the Which Lies only Two Versts from the Convent, When He Saw the Devil in the Shape of a Terrible Monster Creeping out of the Walls. The Beast Hiss'd and Disappear'd with a Dredful Roar.

Bernhard was not the only witness. The same evening several farmers in the area said they had seen the monster. Johann Georg Feverlin also mentioned the reports of other eyewitnesses, who swore that flames had shot out from the body of the beast, its face was misshapen, and it was drinking sheep's blood. The first "witch stories" circulated: people saw lights in the convent at night, and some of the orphan children who lived in the convent became sick with a fever. And so people set out to look for the monster. They didn't in fact find the beast in or near the convent, but the convent burned down anyway—only the walls and the main building remained standing. Gradually there were more and more rumors about the nuns, until a mob set out to search the ruins. Bianca read:

They Found the Chalices with Powder and Unguents that They were Accustom'd to Use When They Did Go Out, Of Which More Stickes with Wild Grotesque Faces and a Flute of Human Bone, on Which a Piper Might Play.

The camera clicked quietly as Nicholas photographed page after page. Finally, the two nuns had to face the accusation that they had consorted with the Devil.

Regina Sängerin did Admit on July 16th that She had even Wish'd to Conjure Up the Monster with the Piper.

She would not admit who the musician was, and so the convent's male employees also fell under suspicion and were interrogated soon afterwards.

It was Claim'd that Hans Haber was a Witch Piper and Did Pipe on the Bone Flute.

"That's the gardener," said Bianca. "I've read about him. And here it mentions Georg Kastellus, the cowherd, too." Fingers trembling, she turned the last page.

...We did Drag the Witch Qveen onto the Windlass and When We Saw Under Her Shirt Her Bare Body, It Had the Mark of the Devil...

The next section was furnished with a symbol that Mrs. Meyer's stepfather had carefully copied from the chronicle.

...a Mark of the Devils Wooing, Burned On with His Kiss.

"That's the mark," said Bianca.

The mark looked like a wolf's head, its fur feathered out behind it like licks of flame.

"And some of the orphan children had it too," Nicholas added. "Look, here's the charge against them."

...the Millers Daughter was Infected and Lam'd by the Witches Children Standing Accus'd.

Two of the "witches' sons" were garroted and then burned at the stake. Bianca and Nicholas read the final sentences with bated breath. Nicholas lowered the camera. "I don't believe it," he whispered. Maybe the hangman's writing in the original documents had been shaky; his words, which his descendant had neatly copied, reported a great commotion and ended with the sentences:

The Witch Qveen and Two of the Others Accus'd Disappear'd. My Servant, Who was Guarding the Prisoners, Awaken'd Lam'd, Without Mark or Injury.

At this point the records broke off, as Mr. Feverlin's grandfather noted matter-of-factly. At the bottom of the page was the date the copy had been made: 7 September 1924.

Bianca and Nicholas looked at each other.

"Maddalina of Trenta was not executed." Nicholas said what they were both thinking. "She got away—and the gardener and cowherd with her."

"And for some reason that's supposed to be kept secret," added Bianca.

The sound of the door opening made them jump, and quickly they turned around. Mrs. Meyer came into the room. "Did you get anywhere? Oh, Martina—don't you feel well? You're quite pale."

"No, I'm fine," replied Bianca, hastily reaching for the photos. "We found a picture of the old manor house at the Europa International School."

"My husband's grandfather was very interested in the building. Apparently it was haunted." Mrs. Meyer laughed. "At that time he belonged to a group that was interested in hypnosis and ghostly visions. But apparently he didn't meet enough spirits there." Now she looked almost mischievous. "Other than perhaps the alcoholic variety, I imagine. Anyway, after the war the Maddalina of Trenta Foundation bought the building, set up the school, and also restored the old orphans' cemetery. If you like I'll ask my stepson. He probably knows more about the school's history."

Nicholas leaned forward to take the photo. As if by chance his glance fell on his watch.

"Oh, goodness, it's getting late," he said. "Mrs. Meyer, thank you so much for everything. I think we have enough information. You were a big help." Without further ado he jumped up and reached for his helmet. Bianca smiled at Mrs. Meyer apologetically. It was rude to break away so suddenly. A few minutes later they were sitting on the motorbike, waving goodbye to Mrs. Meyer.

"Send me a copy of the article!" she called after them.

The lazy afternoon sun hung low in the sky. Nicholas accelerated and Bianca tried not to think what would happen if they did not make a corner. Not too far from the road the river meandered back and forth. When they were still a few miles from the town, Nicholas reduced speed and turned off onto a cart track. Silently they dismounted and walked to the river bank. There they laid the helmets on the ground, sat down beside each other, and looked at the water.

"OK," said Nicholas after a little while. "We have Maddalina, the piper Hans Haber, and Kastellus, the cowherd, who were supposedly burned at the stake."

"And several orphans," Bianca added.

"And don't forget the monster," said Nicholas, continuing her line of thought. "Let's look at the Wolves: they have a nun, a piper, a witch, a girl—and the wolf."

Bianca nodded. "And Joaquim plays the monster."

"Do the Wolves know the true story?"

"Of course," hissed Bianca. "The original chronicle about the witch trial wasn't burned. Someone wrote a new version—that's why the trial seems so superficial and peculiar. And, so no one could check to see if it was genuine, that same someone burned the supposedly original chronicle—except for a few harmless fragments that it's impossible to figure out the whole story from. The rest are only copies. I bet the Foundation is behind it."

"Falsifying history," Nicholas concluded. "Now we need to find out who was in charge of the town archives of the Foundation before the fire."

"Not only before the fire," Bianca replied. "The Wolves have never ceased to exist since Maddalina's time. It's just that no one knew about them until the official founding of the society. They were there the whole time—and they were always involved with things that were illegal or were far ahead of their time." She cleared her throat and quoted: "'the miller's daughter was infected and lamed by the witches' children.'" That could be through hypnosis or suggestion—perhaps with the help of drugs. Experiments like that used to be considered the Devil's work. But the nuns were interested in that sort of thing and obviously knew what they were doing. And in Feverlin's notes it also says that in Maddalina's time chalices and tools were found. Maybe they were tools for making gold. Alchemy—a prohibited science in the middle ages. You could be charged with witchcraft for practicing it."

"I understand," murmured Nicholas. Bianca stared at two ducks chasing each other on the water. She felt sick at the thought of going back to the Wolves' lair today.

"Bianca, what's wrong?" Nicholas's voice broke into her thoughts. Only then did she notice that she had balled her hands into fists and tears were running down her face.

"What's wrong?" Nicholas repeated softly, but she could only shake her head. He did the only thing possible in the circumstances and put his arm around her shoulder. For a while they stared at the water, until Bianca came to a decision.

"Nicholas," she said. "I have to tell you something."

She began at the beginning—with her conversation with her parents on her sixteenth birthday, which had led to her running away in the middle of the night, until she had realized at the bus stop that she had no money and no idea where to go. Then she told him about Alex, who had broken up with her because he did not understand what had changed her so much. She told him about the scholarship that had been advertised at her school, about the exam and her move to the Europa International School. Finally she came to her nightmares, in which Annette Durlain was warning her, and her suspicions about Nemec. Last of all she told him about her latest meeting with Joaquim and Tanja.

"Why didn't you tell me this before?" asked Nicholas. "I'd like to take these guys and whip them within an inch of their lives. They haven't tried anything like that with me so far." He pulled her closer to him. "And now you're feeling guilty that you didn't defend yourself, right? Good heavens, Bianca!"

"As far as your parents are concerned," he said softly after a while, "even if they adopted you, they're still your parents. Or don't you think so?"

"Yes. But since I've known, they seem so foreign to me. How could they pretend all those years that… I feel as if they've been lying to me my whole life. And they wouldn't have told me in a hundred years if I hadn't happened to accidentally find it out myself. I don't even know who my real parents were."

"I know who mine were," said Nicholas. "But it's no help, either—because they're dead. At least you're not alone." He hesitated before continuing. "My mother died when I was five. She was very young—just twenty-six. And my father... just a few months ago."

"I'm so sorry," whispered Bianca.

Nicholas made a dismissive gesture and looked at the river. "I should have told you ages ago. Sorry I didn't tell you the whole truth." He cleared his throat. "I... don't want sympathy."

Bianca bit back the questions that were on her tongue and fell silent.

"DAMN IT, WHERE WERE YOU?" Caitlin berated her. "I thought you'd driven into a ditch somewhere!"

"I'm sorry!" Bianca slipped quickly into the room and threw her unused swimming bag onto the bed. "We went to the Internet café in town afterwards to look something up."

"Your cell phone was off."

Bianca fished her phone out of her jacket pocket. "The battery needs charging," she said contritely. "I didn't hear it beeping."

"Did you find anything out?"

Bianca nodded quickly, went over to her friend, and took her by the shoulders.

"Caitlin, could you call Jenna? The girl who used to be with Tobias?"

"Jenna?" exclaimed Caitlin. "What does she have to do with it?"

"I have to find out whether Tobias has a tattoo on his hipbone. Jenna must know—unless she did nothing with him all year but pick flowers."

"You want me to ring her right now?"

"Please, Caitlin. How else can I find out? Should I drill a hole in the shower walls? Or spill coffee over Joaquim's pants and hope he undresses in front of me?"

"No," Caitlin said dryly. "I really couldn't be responsible for that."

Then she folded her arms and gave a lopsided grin. "Hmm, the Wolves have a tattoo. So I guessed right. You really believed I was one of them?"

Shaking her head, she went into her room, got her cell phone, and looked up Jenna's number.

"Jenna? Hi, it's me, Caitlin. Listen..."

A moment later Bianca took the phone. Jenna's voice sounded far away and a little disembodied. Quickly Bianca explained to her what she wanted to know. Jenna hesitated.

"Do you want something from Tobias?" she asked sharply. "I'd advise you to keep away from him."

"I just want to know if he has a tattoo."

Jenna hesitated again. Bianca bit her lip impatiently.

"Yeah, he does," Jenna replied in a drawl. "It was sort of a test of courage for being accepted into this group..."

"A test of courage?"

Another pause.

"Yes. They tattooed the mark on each other. With an antique needle. He showed me once. Pretty sick, huh? And right where it hurts most."

"Between the hip bone and the belly button—a little closer to the hip."

"Yes. How did you know?"

"What does the mark look like?"

"It's a profile of a wolf's head, with shaggy fur and this kinda creepy tongue. Why do you want...?"

"Thanks, Jenna!" said Bianca quickly, returning the cell phone to Caitlin.

IT

It had found it—there was no longer any doubt: it was here. The strange and yet so familiar Presence, which kept slipping away from It and which It felt compelled to chase after. Its thoughts were calm, and Its claws throbbed under their crusts of blood. For too many hours It had been floating between images and stone, crawling in circles, constantly agitated by the colors, which It could feel and smell like tormenting waves. Faces and eyes went by, and It searched and searched. But now all was still, except for the strange smell nearby. They were breathing in time with each other! It enjoyed the sense of breath flowing, felt the strange warmth, and could hear the comforting sound of blood pumping.

It took Bianca a long time to realize that she was not dreaming any more. The room was dark. She had not fully closed the blinds, so the pale-gray of the parking lot light shone through the slats. Her blue jacket, hanging on the door, looked like an intruder standing in a threatening posture. She had dreamed of a hypnotist, she remembered, closing her eyes again. And about masks. Beside her something was breathing.

BREATHING DEEPLY, it soaked up the scent of the long black fur. Its eyes took in every shadow. No light dazzled It and no color caused It pain; there was just an angular object on which something was lying, something that smelled dry and a little sharp. When It looked more closely, It recognized what the others called "Payper." It was spiteful—it cut. The gray tones of the lump told It that in the light it would be brown. Near the entrance to the cave hung a limp being with two empty arms. It was blue, light blue.

BIANCA OPENED HER EYES again and stared into the darkness. Strangely, she was reminded at this moment of her grandfather's farm dog. He was a very old dog and stank pitifully of musty fur and a little like a damp stable. When she blinked, the images from the first part of her dream flitted by again. What she saw terrified her—dirty children whose horror was burned into their eyes. She looked around—and found herself in a dungeon. It had to be a dungeon, as she was sitting among the children. She could see traces of blood on the walls where their fingers had scratched. And then it was there again—the wolf's mask. "Joaquim!" she murmured, twisting in her bed. The image moved with her. She blinked to get rid of it, but it stayed before her eyes like a nightmare that would not leave its victim in peace. The Wolf raised his hand and removed his mask. She prepared herself for Joaquim's scornful grin.

But it was Nicholas. He looked at her seriously. "At least you're not alone," he said, reaching for her throat. She let him touch her and he did not betray her trust. Gently he stroked her skin. Bianca felt for his hand and recoiled—hard crusts of blood scraped her palm like a rasp. She reached out to Nicholas's face and felt matted hair.

She sat up with a jerk, eyes opened wide. Something was breathing beside her in bed. Caitlin? was her first thought, but then she noticed the smell. A dark, blotchy crack yawned where the mouth should have been. It moved, getting wider and wider—far too wide for a human smile. In spite of the darkness, she could see its teeth.

SHE DID NOT KNOW WHY her throat hurt or why the light was shining in her eyes. It was not until she ran out of air that she stopped screaming. She could feel her jacket pressing into her back and realized that she was standing with her back against the door, staring at the empty bed. Where the thing had lain, there was nothing—just a bulge of pillow that in the darkness had looked like a body lying down. The chair blocking the door handle still stood where she had put it the night before. Caitlin's worried face appeared in the light. With one glance she grasped the situation.

"You were dreaming," she said. "It was just a dream."

The light went on in the hallway and footsteps sounded. There was a knock at Caitlin's door. Gradually the sleepy faces of the students from nearby rooms appeared at the adjoining door. They hardly listened to what Caitlin was telling them. Instead they were eyeing Bianca as if she was crazy.

SECRETS

BIANCA WOKE UP with a plush crocodile in her arms. It took her a while to realize that she was lying in Caitlin's bed. Her friend had puffy eyes. Presumably she, like Bianca, had lain awake in the dark, listening.

"How do you feel?"

"Better," murmured Bianca. Anything was better than lying next to a breathing something with teeth. After Caitlin had gone to take a shower, Bianca got up, too. Nervously, she went to the adjoining door. She had to force herself to open it. Her bed was just as she had left it last night. She was sure that it had not been a case of night terrors, nor a dream. The strange presence had been real. She must call Mrs. Meyer—she would be able to find out more about the ghosts that haunted the old manor house. Quietly, Bianca found her clothes and tried to sort out the debris of the previous day. Before she left, she took her copies and documents and put them in the bottom of one of Caitlin's desk drawers. She took the key with her. There would be time for explanations this afternoon.

THERE WAS NO SIGN of any of the Wolves. For days now they seemed to have been swallowed up by the earth. Jan waved to her once from a distance, as they passed each other in the hallway on their way to different classrooms. Bianca did not go to the physics room to make the call, instead finding a corner in the empty stairwell and pulling out her phone. She misdialed twice before finally getting through.

"Meyer," a quiet, strange voice finally answered. Bianca was so confused that she nearly gave her real name. She caught herself just in time.

"Good morning. This is Martina Huber, from the university magazine," she began. "I'd like to speak to Mrs. Meyer. We were there yesterday. It's about the article..."

In the pause that ensued, Bianca heard the woman at the other end take a deep breath and clear her throat. "Mrs. Meyer... is not available," she said in a hoarse voice.

"Should I try again later?"

The woman hesitated again. "No... you... Mrs. Meyer... died last night very suddenly, of heart failure. The police were here and the doctor is just filling out the death certificate. I'm her neighbor. If your notes are still here, you can pick them up at my..."

Bianca hung up and clutched the phone to her chest. Mrs. Meyer, slim and vigorous, barely fifty, had died of heart failure. This thought was just as strange as the next was terrifying: Who had known about their visit to her? Only her, Nicholas, Jan, and Caitlin. Could Jan have been bought off by the Wolves?

As if her thoughts had echoed throughout the building like a warning siren, she saw a group of students coming around the corner. Tanja! She was talking to another girl, but she could turn her head any minute and see Bianca. Bianca slipped toward the wall. A door handle dug into her hip. She felt for it and fled into the room. The sharp smell of floor cleaner pierced her nose. Holding her breath, she waited until the students' voices faded into the distance. Only then did she dare to turn on the light. It was a storeroom with a cleaning cart. A clear bell announced the beginning of class. Bianca picked up her cell phone with damp fingers.

"Caitlin... Loans Center... Nicholas..." She went through the small list of phone numbers. After a brief hesitation, she pressed the key. She was enormously relieved when someone picked up.

"Hello, Mama?" she whispered. At the other end, the answering machine came on. Bianca fought back tears as she listened to her mother's voice. As always, it sounded gentle and rather monotonous. It felt good to hear it, although longing suddenly overcame Bianca and left her feeling even more lonely. She hung up without leaving a message and called Nicholas.

"The subscriber you are calling is not available at present," said a tinny female voice.

Bianca did not deliberate for long. She rushed into the hallway and ran.

THE BUS INTO TOWN seemed to take forever. The whole way, Bianca felt she was being watched. Several times she turned around, but there was only an old man so engrossed in his newspaper that he had probably missed his stop. Finally the door opened with a hiss. By the time she reached the residence in Pelargus Alley, Bianca was gasping for breath. She tried Nicholas's cell phone one last time, giving full rein to her worst fears: Nicholas kidnapped or killed. She could not find his name on the list at the entrance to the residence, but then she realized that it was only for mail. Nicholas's parents were dead. Presumably he had no one who wrote to him. She remembered that he lived on the third floor, so she ran up the stairs. Music boomed in a narrow hallway. Bianca went from door to door. Not every door had a name on it: some students had made their mark with posters or a cartoon. At the end of the hallway, she reached a small kitchen, where a student in shorts and a crumpled T-shirt was spreading jam on a piece of bread.

"Hi!" called Bianca. "I'm looking for Nicholas Varkonyi!"

The student turned around slowly and squinted in her direction. After a few seconds Bianca's words seemed to register with him.

"Nicholas? Don't know him. But if you mean Niko, he lives one floor up, number 319."

Niko was not Nicholas and did not know anyone of that name. No one knew Nicholas. He did not exist—his description did not even come close to any of the students living in the residence. After half an hour Bianca was in the kitchen again, confused and shaking.

"Hey, sit down a moment," said the student. A bit of jam was stuck to the corner of his mouth. Bianca sank down onto the proffered chair and nodded, as if in a daze, when he asked if she would like a coffee.

"Is he your boyfriend?" the student asked politely. "It sounds like he's really taken you for a ride."

The sympathy in his voice frightened her. She realized that he was right. Nicholas had lied to her. But why? Feverishly she ran through all the possibilities. He'd moved and hadn't told her. He'd given her a false name… the name!

"Klaus Jehle," she said. "He writes for the *Attempto*. Does he live here, at least?"

The student raised his eyebrows and wiped his mouth. "At the other end of the hallway—there's a dream catcher on his door."

Bianca abandoned her coffee cup and rushed out of the kitchen. She hammered vigorously on the door. To her relief she heard movement on the other side of the door. Bedsprings squeaked, something clattered, and then the door opened. A young man with long black hair was looking at her.

Bianca hesitated. "Hello," she finally managed to say. "You… you're Klaus Jehle?"

He folded his arms and looked at her seriously. "That's me," he said laconically. "What's up?"

"I'm looking for Nicholas. Nicholas Varkonyi." Her courage failed her when she saw him wrinkle his brow. "It's about the press card for the *Attempto*," she added.

Finally his expression brightened. "Did this Nicholas find it?"

"You lost it?"

"Yup. A month ago. Or someone stole it." He looked at her suspiciously. "Tell me more," he demanded. "What do you want from me?"

"Nothing. Sorry, I made a mistake." She turned and ran off.

"Hey, wait!" She heard Klaus Jehle's voice behind her, but she did not turn around. Standing in front of the residence, the sun blinding her, Bianca rubbed her damp hands and looked around. Pelargus Alley with its small half-timbered houses and the historic cobblestones looked like a picture frozen in time, a facade behind which a chasm was opening. The face of the dead woman appeared in it—and now Mrs. Meyer's features, too. Bianca had to lean against the wall so as to not lose her balance. She wanted to scream. Damn it, how could she let someone fool her so easily!

The manifestation last night—had it been a warning against Nicholas? Now even the dream with the mask was beginning to take on meaning.

She was in danger; that was the only thing she was certain of. Nicholas was wearing a mask—but what was behind it? Desperately she dug through her pockets for money and found some bills. Too little to simply go to the station and buy a ticket home. The day after tomorrow Madame would return from Brussels. It was time to put the cards on the table. Suddenly it did not matter to her whether she could stay at the school. She just wanted one thing: to be safe, to run away and hide, to forget the disappointment and fear. Just then her cell phone rang. Nicholas. Rage filled Bianca. She pressed so hard on the "Talk" button her fingers hurt. "Leave me alone," she hissed. A few passers-by turned to look at her.

"What's wrong?"

"I've just left your residence. Think about it." With satisfaction she heard him struggling for breath.

"Listen… I can explain."

"Never call me again!"

"Bianca, wait… Please! I've discovered something else. We've got to…"

The display went dark. Bianca had turned the cell phone off.

FINALLY, THE BUS ROUNDED THE CORNER. Bianca, who had found a quiet spot on a park bench in the shadow of a house, jumped up and wiped the tears from her face. She avoided looking across at La Bête, where Nicholas and she had talked for the first time. Brakes screeching, the bus stopped and breathed out with a hiss. The next moment Bianca heard panting behind her. Someone laid a hand on her shoulder. Bianca whirled around and lashed out. Nicholas stumbled backward, his hands pressed to his face. Blood was dripping between his fingers. Behind Bianca the bus drew up. For a moment she saw herself turning on her heels and rushing over to it. It stopped, she got on, and left—from the back window she could see Nicholas getting smaller and smaller, finally disappearing altogether. But the moment passed, and she was still standing in the same spot.

"Oh, shit," groaned Nicholas. "Do you have a handkerchief?"

Bianca shook her head. Strangely, her anger had melted away. What remained was only fear. Nicholas cursed again and pulled up his T-shirt to stop his nosebleed.

"Don't tip your head back," said Bianca.

He glowered at her. "Thanks very much," he mumbled from under the corner of his T-shirt. "Damn it, if I'd known you'd hit me so hard..."

"Then you'd what?" she replied sharply. "Would you have pushed me in front of the bus?" He looked up aghast. "Is that what you did to Annette?" she cried. "Gave her a push?"

"Hey, are you crazy?" he roared.

She pulled back from him and balled her hand into a fist. "I don't know what sort of game you're playing or who you are," she continued more quietly. "But you're not Nicholas—and you don't live in the residence. And I'll bet no professor has set eyes on you at university, either."

He groaned and suddenly looked crestfallen. "You're right," he admitted. "Except for the first. I really am Nicholas."

He reached into the breast pocket of his leather jacket and got out his wallet. His driver's license looked genuine. "Nicholas Varkonyi," it said. His birthplace was given as Kecskemét. And it was true too that Nicholas had turned eighteen just a few months previously. "Please let me explain," he entreated. "I've been wanting to tell you for a long time. And there's something else. I called Mrs. Meyer's house today. She's... dead!"

Bianca, still suspicious, took another step backward. "I know."

Confused, he wrinkled his brow, then looked around as if he was afraid someone had followed him. "Give me five minutes in La Bête," he begged. "On neutral ground."

"You lied to me! The whole story about the Wolves making your life difficult was a lie. You bought my trust with lies!"

She hated herself for sounding so pathetic. Ashamed, he bowed his head.

"Yes, that's true," he said, almost inaudibly. "You seemed so... hard to me, Bianca. At the beginning I didn't like you very much. You were so cold. As if the world wasn't good enough for you. I was just trying to find a way to approach you."

"Well, it worked very well."

"I know. I'm sorry. I didn't want to involve you any more than I had to—five minutes, Bianca. Please!"

NICHOLAS PRESSED THE WET CLOTH the waitress had given him onto the back of his neck. His red nose glowed in his chalk-white face.

Bianca leaned back and folded her arms. "One minute's already gone," she said.

"OK, OK," he snapped. "Can't you drop the arrogance for once?" He pulled himself together and continued, "I'm not a medical student. I just said that so you'd talk to me. I had the feeling you'd be able to tell me more about the school than Jan. He said the Wolves wouldn't leave you alone and so I thought..." He sniffed, then shrugged.

"So, a journalist after all," said Bianca.

He shook his head. "I only finished school last year. And then my father got sick. I looked after him—we have no relatives left, just his distant cousin in Hungary. We lived there for a while."

He cleared his throat and searched for the right words for a long time. Bianca waited while he discarded the cloth, absently fumbled around in his cigarette pack, took out a cigarette, and lit it.

"My father had a stroke," he said hoarsely, blowing out the smoke. "He didn't make it. He died one day after my eighteenth birthday." Again he cleared his throat and blinked a few times too many.

"Well... I had to clear out the house. And I found letters there from my mother. I was five when she died. But I can still remember her laugh. She was a storyteller. Until I was three I believed she was really the Queen of the Clouds and she had fallen into my father's workshop when her horse threw her—and then the next year I was convinced my father was a globe-trotter on the run and she was a Persian princess. She described to me in great detail how my father had carried her off from the palace of the black Sultan. All these stories are almost more real for me than my actual childhood." He took a pull at his cigarette and then stubbed it out again. "She made me believe that we had to hide from the Sultan. That was the only reason we lived in Hungary, and my father had a mustache, so that he wouldn't be recognized. Ever since I've been capable of thought, I've felt as if I'm being followed, and I've tried to keep a low profile. Crazy, huh? She had thousands of stories like that—but I don't know who she really was."

Bianca was still not sure whether to believe him. "And the letters?" she asked.

Nicholas seemed to wake from a daydream.

"The letters, yes. She'd got to know my father when he was living in Budapest and she was on holiday there. For a while they wrote to each other, and then she came to join him in Hungary."

"Did they get married?"

"She didn't want to, although he often asked her. She... she'd been married before, to a man she'd known when she was still at school. The marriage was very unhappy. I found out why from one of the letters."

Nicholas looked as if he'd suddenly come down with a fever. His eyes were glistening. After a pause he continued. "Shortly after her wedding she nearly died," he said quietly. "Because—because her former husband beat her up. When she left him, he threatened to follow her and kill her, wherever she went. She wrote all this to my father—and I didn't understand till a couple of weeks ago why she was always so sad and restless. I think she really spent her whole life hiding from this man. Maybe not well enough."

"Nicholas… that's terrible."

He nodded and took another cigarette from the pack. "She was always frightened something would happen to me. After I'd read her letters I noted the return address and went there. I just wanted to know where she came from and perhaps speak to people who'd known her. Well, I found the address, but a married couple had been living in the house for thirty years. They'd never even heard of my mother. I kept looking, but I didn't find her. It was as if she'd never existed." He sighed. "And then I had one last idea," he said. "In amongst her letters there was a photo. I sat down at the computer and searched for buildings that looked like the one in the background. And I found it. Then I sold everything I'd inherited and came here."

"That's why you have so much money."

"You'd be amazed what's possible when you're willing to fork over a little money. The pathology assistant finds hidden files, Jan builds tools and acts as a spy, and even the cleaning lady at the police station knows where to look. But nothing helped. I still don't know who she really was. She's not on any register. But I came across another name."

"The student."

Nicholas nodded. "He drowned at exactly the same time my mother was here."

"Show me the photo," begged Bianca. He hesitated for a long time. He seemed to find it very difficult to allow her a glimpse into his life. He took out his briefcase again. Carefully he opened a side compartment and took out a small photo. The colors had faded. Bianca thought she felt a crackling between her fingers as she took it. She looked at the picture and understood. The walls of the manor house had not been restored and painted in a light color like today, but she would have recognized it among thousands of buildings. But much more interesting was the girl standing in front of the house. She was wearing a school uniform like the ones Bianca had seen in old pictures in the museum. Light blond hair fell to her shoulders. She looked serious and a little grim, her smile only for the photographer.

Nevertheless you could see that she had a dimple in one cheek. In her arms she was carrying a light-colored leather schoolbag, with two initials burned into the leather.

"How did your mother die?" whispered Bianca.

"She went to Stockholm to visit a friend. She drowned in a ferry accident."

"Was her body ever found?"

He looked at her in amazement, turning even paler. "No," he said. "After ten years she was declared dead."

"What was her name?"

"Klara."

"Klara Varkonyi?"

"Klara Schmidt. She insisted I take my father's last name. Bianca, what's wrong?"

She hitched her chair closer and put her arm around Nicholas. "Listen," she whispered. "I really hope I'm wrong, but I've seen this bag before."

"Where?"

"It was on the floor in Madame Lalonde's office. The day after… the dead woman was found."

His eyes were open so wide that each iris looked like a perfect dove-gray marble. "That means that Madame has the same bag?"

"That means it may well have been one and the same bag," Bianca corrected him. She hated herself for having to tell him the truth. "It means they may well also have been the same person—your mother and Annette Durlain." She indicated the photo lying on the table in front of them. "I can't say if the face is the same. But the dead woman had blue eyes—and a dimple here. She had dark-gray hair, but hair can be dyed. She didn't want to be recognized when she slipped into the school as a tourist."

Nicholas did not seem to have been listening to her properly. Bits of tobacco fell onto the photo and Bianca noticed that he was crushing the cigarette in his hand. "That's impossible," he said. "The dead woman was fifty-four. My mother would only be forty today."

"Forged passport—false date of birth. And of course she made herself look older—a good disguise."

"No," he whispered. "No. It's impossible. I... The autopsy report..." Then he pushed Bianca's hand away roughly and dashed out of the café.

Bianca pulled some money out of her jacket pocket, slammed it onto the table, and ran after Nicholas. To her relief he had not run away. He was standing a few paces away in a side alley, leaning against the house wall, breathing heavily. A few steps, and she was beside him, grasping his shoulders.

"Let's walk a bit," she said. "Show me where you live!"

THE PLACE NICHOLAS WAS REALLY LIVING IN was far less comfortable than the residence. It was on the edge of the old town in a huge unattractive apartment block. Nicholas stumbled through a narrow back door and dragged himself up a never-ending staircase. His room was nothing more than a small attic with a crooked window. There were two suitcases on the floor and a hotplate was perched on an upside-down cardboard box in the corner. The sun had turned the little room into a furnace. Bianca immediately went over to the window and with some effort pushed it open. Nicholas sank down onto the mattress under the sloping ceiling and buried his head in his arms.

"It's impossible," he said finally. "That would mean—that my mother was still alive when I came to town. We may even have walked right past each other in the marketplace..."

"Nicholas, perhaps I'm wrong," said Bianca softly.

"The woman in the photo looks like the woman you saw?"

Bianca gave up trying to be reassuring. "I only saw her for such a brief moment—I can't say for certain. But I'm almost sure it was her. I'm so sorry!"

"Why didn't she ever let me know she was alive? Even after my father's death..."

"She must have wanted to protect you. Don't forget the tattoo—she was one of the Wolves. She even staged her own death so she couldn't be found. She didn't want to get married and she insisted you take your father's name. She herself took the name Schmidt, a name that's very common. In other words, she did everything she could to cover up all traces of you and any connection between the two of you."

"She could have had the tattoo removed."

"Quite likely she tried that. Jenna told me that the Wolves do their tattoos by hand—that usually means they're much too deep. The mark is often still clear even after the tattoo has been removed. The Wolves, at least, were able to recognize the mark. Did you never notice a tattoo or a scar?"

Nicholas had calmed down somewhat. His face set, he sat staring at the wall. After a while he shook his head. "I was only five! When we went to the lake, she wore a swimsuit. No, I don't remember seeing anything."

Dust particles danced in the sunbeams, and from outside the noise of the street reached into the room. Life went on, unmoved and uncaring. Bianca felt as if she were trapped in a block of ice.

"There's something in this school," she whispered. "And it's not just the Wolves—they seem to me to be possessed. Don't think I'm crazy, but I'm beginning to think they practice witchcraft. Think about it: for centuries the Wolves have been experimenting—first with alchemy, then with hypnosis. But always here. Maybe it's a ritual site.

"And my mother's bag is in Madame Lalonde's office. That means she is involved."

Bianca thought for a second, then shook her head.

"The way it looks to me is that the police are in on it—and a couple of the doctors are involved, too. They officially declared the murder to be an accident. If Madame knows about that, it would make sense for her to hide the bag from the police. And also, she's trying to find new sponsors for the school right now. If Joaquim's father has something to do with the murder, that would make sense, too: she'll get the school's financing in order before handing over the evidence."

Nicholas ran his hands through his hair. "We'll break into her office," he said dully. "Today. I'll call Jan."

"No!" said Bianca, almost shouting. "That would be too dangerous. If the Wolves killed Mrs. Meyer, then they'll be watching me all the more closely now. No, we'll wait until Madame comes back."

"Do you really think that's a good idea?"

"It's just two days."

Doubtfully Nicholas looked at her. Finally he nodded in defeat.

"I'll sleep here," she said. "I wouldn't be able to get a wink of sleep at school. Is it OK with you if I go to the school one more time? I'll just get my things. I'll be back in an hour." She sat down on the bed beside Nicholas and hugged him. He hesitated for just a moment, then hugged her back.

"No more secrets."

"No more secrets," whispered Nicholas.

A HAZY, COLORLESS SKY behind the school gave the effect of a black and white photo. Today the buildings looked terrifying in their modernity. After hesitating briefly, Bianca entered the school. Inside, her steps quickened until she was running up the stairs to her dorm. Surprised faces flashed past her. Finally she was at her own door, searching frantically for her keys. She didn't notice the envelope until she had unlocked the door. The school's office stamp was emblazoned on it. Bianca tore the envelope open and read the letter. A summons because of unexcused absences. In her room, everything was as she had left it. She had expected to find her drawers ransacked. With a sigh of relief she looked at the clock—Caitlin would not be back for an hour. Bianca pressed down the handle of the adjoining door and went into her friend's room. She looked around in disbelief. Caitlin was gone. Not only Caitlin—everything that had belonged to Caitlin. The bare mattress lay on the bed.

The chair, desk, and dresser stood abandoned against the wall. The little pinholes in the walls from Caitlin's posters and pictures were the only evidence that she had ever lived there. For a strange moment it seemed to Bianca that her friend had never really existed. She pulled her cell phone out of her pocket and switched it back on. Before she could dial Caitlin's number she saw there were ten beeps, telling her she had missed a lot of calls. All of them Jan. Heart thudding anxiously, Bianca waited for Caitlin to pick up. There was a click, then a mechanical voice announced that the subscriber could not be reached.

"Damn!" The word slipped out. Her eyes filled with tears. She reached into her pocket for a tissue. Something fell out and landed on the floor with a clatter. The key to Caitlin's desk. Bianca sniffed back her tears, picked up the key, and went over to the drawer. It was still locked. The key turned easily. Bianca pulled the drawer open. Empty.

SHE COULD SEE that it was Jan calling. However, when she picked up, she would never have known. His voice sounded thin and worried.

"Bianca! Finally! Did you talk to Caitlin?"

"No—I don't even know what's going on. Her things have gone, and..."

"She didn't pass the exam."

"What?"

"It's on the list on the notice board. I thought she wasn't answering her phone because she was frustrated, but then someone in her class told me she left this afternoon." He paused, struggling for breath. "I don't believe it—she didn't even say goodbye to me. And that she didn't pass..."

"Can't be true," said Bianca, finishing his sentence.

"Where is she?"

Dead? thought Bianca. She rushed out of the empty room, slammed the adjoining door shut, and leaned her back against it. Now alarm bells sounded in Jan's voice. "Bianca, are you crying?"

"Of course I'm crying," Bianca snapped. "I dragged her into this—damn!"

"Dragged her in? What do you mean? Are you in your room? I'm coming right over!"

Bianca slid down the smooth door and wrapped her arms around her knees. After the shock, it took her a minute to think of calling Nicholas.

"I'm sure she didn't fly back to Ireland just like that, without telling anyone," she stammered into the phone. "She must still be somewhere in the school."

Nicholas thought for a moment. She was amazed that he could remain so calm.

"We'll look for her—tonight."

METROPOLIS II

"TAKE THE LAMP," whispered Jan. When the flashlight's beam flitted over his face, Bianca could see his cheeks glowing. He was screwing an adapter onto his lock opener, while Nicholas, following his instructions, unrolled a cable. Nicholas was limping a little. When they had climbed in through the chemistry lab window past the alarm system, with Jan's help, he had stumbled and knocked his injured leg again. It was now 2:30 in the morning. It had taken Jan more than half an hour to disarm the alarm system at the door to the office area. Finally the door opened with a hum. The equipment Jan was using today was not a small door-opener—it was a strange-looking machine that bore some resemblance to a mixer. In the weak beam of the flashlight Bianca saw wires and the uneven surfaces of small soldered metal plates, holding various connections.

In single file they crept along the passage leading to the headmistress's office and staff rooms. They stopped in front of Madame's door. Jan nodded to them and indicated to Nicholas to plug in the cable.

"Are you sure we need to break into her office?" he whispered. Bianca nodded.

"The school archives are in her room—and there's a adjoining door to the school office."

"But Caitlin won't be there."

"No, but we need a starting point. There must be a floor plan or a calendar there. Something." And, she said to herself, maybe there's also some trace of Nicholas's mother. Jan wiped his hand over his forehead and pushed a pin into the keyhole. The machine hummed again, then there was a screeching noise.

"Shit!" whispered Jan.

"What's wrong?"

Carefully he pulled the pin out again. A scratch gleamed in the metal.

"Wrong key," he growled. He reached into his pants pocket and took out a much stronger pin.

"Don't be scared," he said softly. "Something's going to break in a moment. Move back."

Obediently, Bianca took a step to the side. The next moment there was a loud hum, then there was silence, until they heard a dreadful grinding noise. The door swung open. Bianca stared in horror at the hole and the splinters of wood.

"The door's broken," Nicholas stated.

"So what?" Jan turned on him. "I'd like to burn the place down with them in it! They've done something with Caitlin and you're worrying about a door?"

Nicholas raised his hands. "Hey, calm down," he said. "Don't yell like that here!"

Bianca stretched out her hand and laid it on Jan's shoulder. "It's all right, Jan. We'll find her."

He nodded and wiped his hands on his pants.

"Are we going in, or what?"

"Yes. Let's go!" Bianca led the way. Like shadows they flitted into the office and pushed the armchair in front of the door. Nicholas let down the blinds. Only then did they dare to turn the little flashlight back on. The beam of light roamed over the bookcases and was reflected in the glossy bindings of thick books. It was not long before Jan had the first of Madame's desk drawers open. The headmistress was an exceptionally tidy person. Everything, every sheet of paper, every pencil, was placed meticulously. Bianca felt guilty snooping around. They found only notebooks containing accounting records, receipts for books on financial management, and a copy card.

"To the office," whispered Bianca. In the sparse light Nicholas's face made her think of a wax death mask.

In the office they had a lot more to search through. Mountains of files and loose papers were heaped at the edge of the gigantic table. Bianca brought out the second flashlight and began sifting.

"Maybe we should start with the computer," said Nicholas after a little while.

Jan, who had been searching a desk drawer, stood up suddenly, bumping his shoulder against the desk chair.

"I've found something," he hissed. In grim triumph he held up a folder. "Here!"

They crowded into the light and stared at the long rows of numbers.

"According to this list, Caitlin got an even worse mark in mathematics than Michael Cline," Bianca declared.

"They've killed her!" Jan burst out.

"Don't jump to conclusions," said Bianca, pulling Jan up by his arm. "Quick, into Hasenberg's office!"

She did not want to admit that she was beginning to lose heart.

She felt even more nervous as they entered Hasenberg's domain.

"What are we waiting for?" whispered Nicholas. Jan grabbed his machine and plugged it in. Here the search was more difficult. Inside the cabinets were more compartments, each with its own lock. In most cases they were special locks, and Jan, cursing, tried different pins until they finally yielded to the steel teeth of his lock breaker. Bianca found dozens of sketches that looked like geometric diagrams. She recognized them easily —they were family trees. Behind her she heard the crunch of a pane of glass breaking. Jan swore quietly.

"Bianca!" The stifled cry made her turn around quickly. Nicholas was standing in the middle of the room. At first she thought he was swaying, but then she realized that it was the flashlight, which he had put down on the table. It was rolling back and forth as if drunk. It was not until the beam of light slid back that she recognized what Nicholas had taken from a compartment of the shelf with the broken glass.

"The bag!"

Dazed, Jan squinted into the light. "What sort of bag?"

"The proof," replied Nicholas bleakly. Bianca could see his face contorting. She jumped up and went to him. The bag still felt soft and almost familiar. Together they laid it carefully on the floor. "M. J." Nicholas quietly read the initials aloud. "There's the clue to her real name."

Bianca resisted the temptation to reach out to the clasp. The bag belonged to Nicholas now. Gingerly, he touched the front. His fingers left dark marks in the suede. The clasp opened with a soft clink. Nicholas turned the bag over and emptied it out onto the floor. The dead woman had not carried very much around with her: a knife with an ivory handle and an old-fashioned 35mm camera. Nicholas popped open the case and shook his head. "No film," he whispered. In a side pocket there were several sheets of thick paper. Nicholas unfolded them and laid them on the carpet. Carefully he stroked them flat.

"A map. Do you know what it's of?"

Bianca slid across the carpet to look at the map so quickly that her knees burned. It was the floor plan of a huge building. Only one room on the east side seemed vaguely familiar to her. It was outside the building, separated by a long passage. A few lines indicated stairs.

"The single room is the basement of the museum," she said quietly. "This square here is the display case with the witch's robe. And the small square is the piece of the old convent door that's hanging on the wall."

"A door?" whispered Nicholas.

"The door behind the door," Bianca amended. "*Porta post portam*—the school's motto. The door leads to a building underneath the school."

Nicholas laughed softly and shook his head. "You were right," he said hoarsely. "The school, the teachers—the students—it's all just superficial. Madame and the scholarships, the teachers—all puppets in a puppet theater. The real world lies below the surface. And my mother knew that."

"Hey!" came Jan's sharp whisper from the other corner of the room. "Take a look at this!"

Bianca and Nicholas jumped up together. Jan slapped a transparent folder onto the table. Accusingly he shone the flashlight onto it.

"Here's Caitlin's test. Not marked. I bet it was an A+."

"The mark behind the mark," said Nicholas. "The door behind the door."

"Someone must be damned good at copying handwriting," said Bianca. "Perhaps the same person who wrote the new version of the convent chronicle." And, she added to herself, my messed-up history exam.

THE BACK STAIRS THAT JAN USED to lead them to the museum were steep and narrow.

When they entered the hallway again and Bianca saw a red light blinking, she nearly gave up hope. "This one's a really big alarm system," she whispered. "There's one like it in the town museum. Do you think you can deal with it?"

She could not see Jan's expression, but she could tell by the way he shrugged his shoulders that he was up for the challenge. Without another word he took something out of his pocket. There was a click, and then the red light dimmed, finally going out altogether. The flashlight went on. Astounded, Bianca looked at Jan. "You have a remote control for the alarm system?"

"And for the video camera over the door," he replied.

"And what's on the tape now?"

"The still image of an empty museum," Jan replied dryly.

Bianca and Nicholas were amazed when they saw Jan walking in as if he were following his daily route to school.

The witch's robe glimmered eerily in the beam of the flashlight. The overhead light snapped on. Bianca and Nicholas recoiled, huddling against the wall. Jan, who was standing by the light switch, looked at them in amusement.

"What's wrong?" His voice echoed. "Nobody's here—it's hermetically sealed. So it's OK to have the light on."

"You come here a lot, do you?" Nicholas was pale. Bianca took his hand, which felt cold and dry.

"Could be." Jan went over to a piece of wood paneling that had an almost invisible groove cut around it. Skillfully he took hold of it and lifted up a flap. Thick cables and power meters came into view.

"The school's main junction box," he said. "Do you see the ceramic fuses?"

Bianca was wide-eyed. "The power cut we had the other day," she said. "That was you?"

"Only happened once," he replied. "Then I had it under control. What door are you talking about? The old ruin back there?"

THE FRAGMENT of the old convent door on the wall towered in front of them like the jagged, blackened tooth of a dragon. Bianca had to force herself just to touch the ancient wood. Nicholas and Jan gripped it by the edges.

"On three," commanded Nicholas. The door creaked a little in its iron brackets but hardly moved. Then, when their hands were getting slippery from sweat, it started to move with a screech. The whole time Bianca had the feeling that the wooden apostles on the door were eying them reproachfully. Once she even thought she heard a thin cry through the wall—Caitlin's voice? The screech became a squeak as the door suddenly slid out of its supports and swung to the side, surprising them.

"A hinge," Jan confirmed calmly. "And a hydraulic system. Man, we only needed to lift it and push!"

Amazed, Bianca and Nicholas looked at what should have been wall. Instead there was a narrow metal door.

"The door behind the door," whispered Bianca.

"Not a chance," Jan said, with a professional glance at the lock. "Latest generation security lock. I can't open that with my master key."

"Does that mean we have to give up?" Nicholas asked angrily.

Jan's eyes flashed. "Do it look like I'm giving up?" He cracked his knuckles, staring at the lock as if it was his enemy. "For this I need Metropolis II, from the art room."

THE FEATURES of the floor plan were firmly fixed in Bianca's memory by the time she finally heard footsteps and a rumbling sound. She slid the map under her shirt and jumped up in relief. She had spent the past quarter of an hour sitting with her back against the wall, memorizing. Only the center part was drawn completely—she could not tell whether the passageways that were indicated at the sides led to other rooms or were just exits. Nicholas's red face appeared. Together he and Jan dragged a machine into the room. It looked like something out of a science-fiction film. A tangled mass of cables and stiff hoses hung over Jan's shoulder. Carefully they set down the machine. Nicholas stood up and stretched his sore leg.

"The thing's made of lead," he groaned.

"Steel," Jan corrected him. "It operates at 3000 psi. If it was lead, the cables would fly all over the place."

"So it works on pressure?"

"Of course. You know the jaws of life that firemen use? This is the same principle. An electric motor using 400 volts AC and an oil-pressure pump that creates pressure. You can open pretty well anything with it. And as it's a hydraulic system, it hardly makes any noise. I've tested it several times on the furnace power supply." He reached into his pants pocket and pulled out a cylindrical piece of metal. He quickly pushed it into the keyhole of the main door of the museum and used a small key to lock it.

"Special plug-in lock for security locks," he explained. "Without this key no one can open the door. We don't want any surprise guests coming into the Convent Museum tonight, do we?"

Jan unscrewed the front and side panels of Metropolis II, a block that looked like a car battery with levers and a cylinder screwed onto it. Bianca looked over at two hydraulic pry bars that were vaguely reminiscent of a pair of scissors. Jan reached for the thick cables and pressure hoses. Calmly he began to hook up his machine and to attach the power cables underneath the ceramic fuses. Nicholas sat down beside Bianca and passed her a cloth in which several hard objects were wrapped.

"I only have my pocketknife with me," whispered Nicholas. "But I'm sure these'll be better — they were in the art room."

Shuddering, Bianca looked at the sharp blades of the box cutters sticking out of the cloth.

Jan noticed her worried face and grinned. "Nothing can go wrong," he explained, indicating his Metropolis machine. "The motor turns itself off if necessary. Idiot-proof. Give me a hand, Nick!"

It took a couple of minutes before the machine was positioned properly in front of the door. With intense concentration, Jan jammed the pry bars between the door and the steel frame.

"OK!" he cried. Bianca expected at any minute to hear an earsplitting explosion and then to feel splinters driving into her back. Instead there was an ugly metallic grinding sound.

Shortly afterwards the door, bent completely out of shape, swung open. Nicholas whistled appreciatively.

"There really are stairs," whispered Jan.

The smell emanating from the narrow stair shaft of the secret passageway was reminiscent of a deep cellar where wine bottles indulge in their dusty dreams of Christmas parties and clinking glasses.

Bianca could not help thinking of Caitlin, tied up and mistreated, being dragged into this tomb. She picked up a box cutter in her right hand and the flashlight in her left. At every step the papers that she had slid under her T-shirt rubbed against her skin.

Bianca counted each stair. Behind her she could hear Nicholas breathing fast. From one stair to the next the air grew cooler. The passage walls seemed to be getting closer and closer together. Bianca imagined she could hear the echo of her own heartbeat. Finally the end of the stairs came into view. Calves aching, they entered an even narrower passageway. Bianca closed her eyes, mentally tracing their route so far, working from the approximate distance and the number of stairs, and relating it to the length of the passageways on the floor plan.

"Thirty yards straight ahead and then right," she said quietly.

The passageway was so narrow that they could only go through in single file. Bianca went first, trying not to think about what she might meet. The passageway was paneled with wood and smelled of fresh varnish. A light breeze brushed Bianca's cheeks in passing—somewhere there must be an air conditioner.

They turned off, following the curve of another passageway. It suddenly ended. Bianca stopped so abruptly that Nicholas jostled against her. Silently Bianca let the beam of her flashlight roam upward. They were standing in front of a stone passage. Relief sculptures bordered the doorway on both sides—sculptures of wolves hunting.

"That's old," whispered Bianca. "It must be even older than Maddalina's convent."

Quietly they walked through the doorway and entered an underground cathedral. A graceful gothic vault rose above them, designed in a way that made it able to bear a great weight. Awestruck, they looked around.

"So this is where Maddalina and the others fled to," whispered Bianca. "They simply disappeared—through a secret passage into the underground convent."

"Where next?" Jan urged.

Bianca shut her eyes and visualized the plan. "At the back on the right some other passageways branch off."

Wide-eyed, they ran through stone passages where ancient sculptures sat in niches. These were not figures of saints but the faces of mortals that looked like chiseled death masks. At a fork in the passage, Bianca looked over at one niche and recoiled in horror.

"Oh my God!" whispered Nicholas. Two skulls were grinning at them.

Bianca turned the flashlight's beam onto the ceiling. A root protruded between two stones. The orphans' cemetery is above us," she said.

"Wrong," came Jan's dry answer. "The cemetery is down here." He pointed to other niches, where several skulls lay, as if in a catacomb.

"If there are no dead bodies up there in the coffins, then what's in them?" whispered Nicholas.

"I couldn't care less," replied Jan. "Where's Caitlin?"

The fear in his voice infected Bianca. The passageway got

wider again and became an oval room. Stopping all at once, they stumbled and grabbed for each other. Several heavy wooden doors appeared in the flashlight's trembling beam. They were small and almost square, about four feet high. The top of the one on the right of the passageway was pointed. There could be anything behind them: a burial chamber, a passage, Hell, or—a prison. The bolt closing this door from the outside was shut. Before Bianca could stop him, Jan ran to the door and hammered on the wood.

"Caitlin?" he called softly. There was a rumbling noise, and then someone moved on the other side of the door.

Every hair on Bianca's body stood up. "No, Jan!" she cried, dashing to the door. Jan spun around. It was not until the floor came up to meet her that Bianca realized that Jan had pushed her aside roughly and that she was falling. She hardly felt the impact. The bolt slid back with a scraping sound.

"Caitlin!" Jan cried, flinging the door open.

AT THIS MOMENT, which seemed everlasting, Bianca learned two things. One, that it took only a fraction of a second to be catapulted out of the world of formulas and hypotheses forever. The other, that reality could be worse than any nightmare. The creature that crawled out of its room into the light of the flashlight could not be real. Pale limbs groped their way over the stone. Glittering eye slits were surrounded by predatory folds, and the mouth became wider and wider. The beam of light moved over the grotesque face. Terrified by the light, the monster let out a shrill cry and then sprang aside with a repulsively agile movement. Claws scraped over stone like chalk over a slate board, and then all sound ceased, even the panting breath. The creature had discovered Bianca. For a moment, time stood still. For one confusing moment Bianca thought she could see two Nicholases—the one she knew and the one in the mask, the wolf mask, a mask that was now baring its teeth triumphantly. Nicholas sprang up at the same instant as the creature, and then the shadows came. With a dull thud Bianca's flashlight fell to the floor and went out. Bianca turned and ran. Her own panting drummed in her ears, drowning out Jan's and Nicholas's voices, which fell farther and farther behind. But the scraping noise behind her was much louder, the raw breath getting closer and closer. Bianca screamed when she brushed against a wall with her shoulder, felt an archway, the wall of a hallway, and a skull that rolled away under her hands and shattered with a dry crash. The creature was faster than she was, much faster. In her mind's eye she could see it pursuing her, bounding like a lion. Far ahead there was a glimmer of light. When Bianca felt the almost loving touch of claws on the back of her knee, she forgot the light and just ran. Then she felt two arms wrapping themselves around her and a bandaged mummy-like hand pressing her lips painfully against her teeth. She squinted into the darkness, but the monster seemed to have disappeared. "You're frightening him," a rough voice whispered into her ear. The smell of alcohol was overpowering.

"If I let you go, will you be sensible?" asked Simon Nemec. Bianca pressed against his hand, hoping he would interpret the movement as a nod. He released her. Nearby a match was struck. Concerned, Nemec wrinkled his brow, but he was not looking at Bianca. His glance was drawn to where a whimpering sound was coming from. Bianca reached out for the uneven wall, braced herself against it, and turned around, trembling.

The monster sat huddled against the wall, rocking back and forth, as if trying to soothe a pain.

"You kicked him," Nemec rebuked her.

"It... it attacked me," Bianca replied. She watched in bewilderment as the janitor bent down and stroked the creature's matted hair comfortingly with his bandaged hand. The monster raised its head and looked at Bianca despondently. It had blue eyes, she saw. Not a predator's eyes. Like a blind person who finally understands what he has been touching, she realized what the monster was. It had been searching for her all along—it had felt for her in its thoughts and had finally found her. And it was a human being. A young man. His skin was very pale, as if he had not seen the sun for many years. His claws were long, horny fingernails. His shoulder bore several barely healed cuts in the pattern of a spider's web. His head hung forward, making him look even more like an animal. What Bianca had thought of as predatory folds were tattoos. Black lines depicting a beast of prey had been drawn on his face, making it look like that of a wolf. The young man looked at Bianca and contorted his face. It pained her to see him trying to smile at her. His molars gleamed. Bianca felt so nauseated that she slid down the wall and covered her face with her hands. Apparently a long time ago someone had slit open the corners of the man's mouth to make him look more like an animal.

"Who did that to him?" whispered Bianca. Nemec shrugged, took a candle from a niche by the door and lit it with the dying match.

"Maddalina, Hans Haber, Joaquim—all of us." His voice shook. "And that means me too."

"The Wolves, then," she said. "And you're one of them."

"Yes, and sometimes no," returned Nemec. Apprehensively

he looked round. "Not at the moment, otherwise you wouldn't be standing here asking me questions."

"Would I end up like him?" Bianca replied bitterly. "What did he do?"

Nemec's face softened as he looked at the boy. "It's his destiny. He knows nothing else, Bianca. He's a wolf-child; he grew up without human contact. Light hurts him, but in the darkness he can even distinguish colors. He hardly feels heat and cold. His senses are sharper than ours—they're so finely tuned that he can even see the colors of our thoughts."

"That means you locked him up down here when he was just a child," gasped Bianca. "You're all crazy!"

Nemec's gaze seemed to smolder in his somber face. "In a way it makes him freer than any of us," he whispered. "He doesn't know who or what he is. He's a wolf—with all the capabilities of a man. With all the intuition and powers that most men lost centuries ago. Haven't you felt it, Bianca? His presence is everywhere!"

Bianca looked at the wolf-man. Thinking exhausted her; she felt as if her whole body was trembling. "Then he's a... medium," she whispered.

Nemec swayed slightly and reached out to the wall to steady himself. "In a way, yes," he said, his voice rough. "He picks up our thoughts subconsciously. In his mind he can go wherever he wants." He laughed as if he had made a joke.

"Are you drunk?" Bianca tone was accusing.

Immediately Nemec grew serious again. "Down here is the only place it's possible to think clearly," he growled. "Thoughts vanish into the mist—and the others can't understand them."

"Can the Wolves?"

Something like pride lit up his face. "Belverina's gift. We had it once and we'll have it again. For centuries they tried to take it away from us, but the Wolves are learning—they're learning again and transforming themselves."

The wolf-man let out a soft sound.

Simon Nemec froze. "He hears them," he whispered. "They're going into the assembly room." Bianca did not pull back when he grasped her by the shoulders. He no longer seemed aware of his injured hand. "They mustn't find you!" He pushed her roughly and ran off. Without stopping to think she stumbled after him, through dark passageways—it seemed like the same route she had taken on the way here. The round beam of a flashlight confirmed her guess. Nemec almost fell when he saw two figures coming around the bend. Bianca could see Jan's eyes gleaming, wide with fright.

"Don't ask questions," she hissed. "Come on!"

The wolf-man was running beside her on all fours; she could feel his breath on her hand. Nemec was heading back to the room from which they had freed the wolf just a few minutes before, running so fast that his jacket billowed out behind him. He pushed the door open. "What are you waiting for?" whispered Nemec. "They won't look for you here!"

Bianca hesitated, looking into the janitor's watery eyes. She could hear footsteps approaching in the distance. She imagined Joaquim and the other Wolves getting nearer.

"Come on!" she commanded Nicholas and Jan. They looked at each other doubtfully, but Bianca took their hands and dragged them along behind her. The wolf-man made a plaintive sound and did not move an inch. Only when he saw Bianca go in did he follow. Nemec slid the bolt across on the outside.

"Are you crazy?" whispered Jan.

"Shut up, otherwise we're finished!" Bianca ordered. It

smelled like Mrs. Meyer's living room—of animal fur and tanned hides. Except that the smell was a hundred times stronger. They could hardly hear anything at all through the door: just murmuring and Nemec's grumpy voice in response. Frightened, they waited, huddling close together. After a while Bianca raised her head and looked around. Light came from a tiny lamp in a niche. Animal furs lay on the floor, and some were rolled up against the wall. All around, the walls were covered in scratch marks that looked like outlandish cave paintings. How many hours must the wolf-man have spent searching for a way out of his prison?

The door swung open and Nemec slipped into the room. "Come on! I'll show you the way."

"Not without Caitlin!" hissed Jan.

Nemec stared at him in astonishment, then he broke into hoarse laughter. "You came here because of the Irish girl?"

"She's disappeared."

Nemec made a dismissive gesture. "She went home. I took her to the airport myself. She was told that Bianca was being expelled too."

"Why?"

"Copies were found in her room. She was careless enough to say they belonged to you, Bianca. Anyone who breaks into the bookroom and makes copies runs the risk of being expelled."

"And you had the key to Caitlin's room?"

"Oh, no," Nemec replied anxiously. "Not me. I don't have any keys to the students' rooms. But in this case no key was needed. You were clever enough to lock your room, Bianca. Caitlin forgot this time."

"How do you know I lock my room?" Bianca's mouth was hanging open. "Oh," she said, it all making sense now. "It was you, the night the power went out. You tried to get into my room!"

"I only checked to see if your door was locked. It's better to keep the doors locked when the Wolves have decided to do battle."

"I had the key to the drawer!"

"It's not hard to open a drawer like that, with a piece of wire, for example."

"You're lying to us!" cried Jan.

The cowering wolf-man growled and straightened up. Nicholas crawled away as fast as he could, to keep as much distance as possible between himself and the wolf.

"He isn't lying, Jan," said Bianca.

"Give me one reason why I should trust him," returned Jan.

"I won't give you any reasons. I'll just get you out of here, nothing more," said Nemec.

"Annette Durlain trusted you, didn't she?" Nicholas's knuckles were white—he was gripping the box cutter so tightly.

Nemec turned slowly in his direction.

"Maybe she was called Klara Schmidt, too," Nicholas added. "Did you kill her?"

The wolf-man was oblivious, gazing at Nicholas.

"Well?" Nicholas gasped. "Did you kill her?"

The wolf-man began to bare its teeth in imitation of Nicholas's rage.

Bianca had to look away.

"I don't know who you mean," said Nemec coolly.

"I mean the woman who was found dead at the foot of the stairs."

Nemec and Nicholas eyed each other for a long time.

"Meret Johanna Vargas," murmured Nemec finally. "We just called her Johanna. No, I didn't kill her. I would never have done that. Never!" He fell silent and made a sound that sounded like a stifled sob.

"What was she looking for?" asked Bianca quietly.

Nemec sighed and wiped his eyes with the back of his hand. He cleared his throat and pointed toward the wolf-man, who had stopped baring his teeth.

"Her son," he said softly. "She wanted to rescue him. I was keeping watch... That evening was the perfect time. The Wolves were distracted, taking the new students around. We just had to wait until the orphans' cemetery was empty. But Johanna..."

The box cutter fell to the floor.

"That's not true," whispered Nicholas. "I'm her only child."

Bianca took a step toward him. Now the incident in her room, when she felt a presence next to her and had dreamed of Nicholas behind a wolf mask, was making sense. Nemec held his head in his hands and slid down the wall until he was sitting on the stone floor.

"So it's true," he said to Nicholas. "She told me about you. I just never took it in."

"She abandoned me for his sake," said Nicholas. Bianca had expected him to be upset, maybe fall apart completely, but he was quite calm.

"She left you to protect you," Nemec corrected him. "It was very hard for her to do that. But she managed to make herself invisible. When she ran away all those years ago, even I thought she was dead."

"And she simply left the wolf... her child... behind?" asked Bianca.

Nemec laughed bitterly. "She was just a child herself. She was seventeen when she got pregnant—in eleventh grade. By a student."

"The one who drowned," whispered Nicholas.

Nemec nodded.

"It was against the Wolves' rules, because he wasn't one of us. Johanna was descended in a direct line from Maddalina and Hans Haber."

Suddenly Bianca felt stupid. She remembered all the hours she had spent brooding over the chronicles of the witch trial. The answers had been right in front of her nose the whole time! "So the nuns actually had children themselves," she realized. "The witches' sons. And where can you hide children without anyone noticing? In an orphanage."

"Oh, there were genuine orphans, too," said Nemec. "Maddalina wasn't stupid. But it didn't help. The children who weren't condemned and killed at the time of the witches' trial left town and scattered all over the world. But the Wolves searched for them—and they're still searching for them today. All over the world. And often enough, they find them." He smiled grimly. "Except for Johanna—Johanna was the best of all. She became invisible. And her second son seems to have inherited this talent from her."

"What did the Wolves do to her?" asked Nicholas in an expressionless voice. He still could not tear his gaze away from the wolf. "How did... he..." He fell silent. The pale-skinned boy stared back.

"For centuries a wolf has always lived within the walls. He has to be here. It's an old place, a mythical place, one that holds the soul of many centuries. As long as the wolf lives, so also do the Wolves, and their memories of the dead. But the wolf had grown old. Its thoughts had begun to fade. Its end was drawing near. Before it could be killed, a new wolf must be chosen: Johanna's child. For a long time she didn't want to accept it.

She thought she could simply say "No, thanks" and leave. Then, when her boyfriend drowned, she understood." Nemec sighed. "She didn't manage to save her child, but she herself fled. To us she was dead. She hid. She moved around and changed identities so often that she herself often hardly recognized the face in her mirror. But she never forgot her wolf-child. She spent years making all the preparations—she laid trails and created escape routes. And when she contacted me a year ago and told me she was ready to come and get him, I..." He swallowed hard.

"... helped her." Bianca finished his sentence. "You sent her the floor plan. The timing was perfect. She dyed her hair, made herself look older, and went to see the exhibits, masquerading as a tourist. It was the day the new students arrived—good timing again, because that meant the Wolves were busy. She didn't leave the school—she stayed in the building."

"It was crazy," whispered Nemec. With difficulty he rose from the floor and wiped his mouth. "I gave her the key to the museum door—and she went and got her son. But as she was about to flee..." He shook his head as if trying to drive out the memory. "I didn't know that the Wolves had locked the exit to the orphans' cemetery. She turned around and was going to escape through the exhibit room."

"Where the Wolves found her and killed her," finished Bianca. "Did they do this to the wolf-man?" she inquired, pointing to the cuts across his back.

"He ran into the display case. Although he had a fever and the wound wasn't healing, he couldn't let go of Johanna—he looked for her, and he found her—in your thoughts, Bianca."

"That's why I heard footsteps."

Nemec nodded. "Echoes—a lot of people with Belverina's gift hear them. This is an old place. Maybe they're really echoes of the past. That kind of haunting usually occurs with someone who isn't aware of causing such incidents. And the prophetic ability is usually particularly strong in such people."

"Why didn't you free him yourself?" whispered Nicholas.

"I'm not like Johanna," replied Nemec with resignation. "I never was. I can only be different when I'm drunk. How often can you get drunk? And where could I have taken him? Where could I go myself? I'm a Wolf. They'd have found me, wherever I was." He hesitated. "Anyway, I'd only be going from one prison to another. They have me in their power. Forging documents isn't a minor crime, particularly when you're talking about contracts."

"You were the one who forged the chronicles—and some exams. All on the Wolves' orders."

"Not all." He smiled bitterly. "I forged your exams so you wouldn't be accepted. They only take the best."

"You stole my notes so you could practice my handwriting. And so the Wolves wouldn't suspect, you bandaged your hand so it wouldn't occur to anyone that you could write forged exams in that condition."

The wolf-man raised his head and listened. "Go," Nemec urged. "Take him with you—maybe you'll have more luck than Johanna!"

Bianca went over to the wolf-man and stroked his hair. She did not know whether he understood her words, but he would know what she meant. "Come with me," she said softly.

THE FLAME OF NEMEC'S CANDLE floated ahead of them in the darkness like a beacon. As quietly as possible they made their way through the passageways. The wolf-man had the least difficulty. He moved so quickly and surely on all fours that it startled Bianca. The passageways narrowed again. They crossed two chambers and came at last to a narrow aluminum staircase that rose steeply.

"Up there," Nemec ordered. Without hesitation Bianca grasped the handrail and pulled herself up. Above her head she discovered a hatch bolted shut. When she glanced down, she saw their four faces looking up at her. Nemec gestured impatiently. Bianca nodded and reached for the bolt. As if just thinking about it caused it to happen, it snapped back. Confused, she pulled her hand away. The hatch swung open. Joaquim's face appeared. Thinking quickly, Bianca reached up and grabbed hold of his fur collar. Joaquim swayed a little but did not fall. Something hard hit Bianca's hand, sending bolts of pain shooting up into her shoulder. The faces below her started to spin—and she fell.

CORDS CUT INTO HER WRISTS. From time to time Tanja jabbed her between the shoulder blades, driving her on. Bianca had lost all sense of where they were a long time ago. Their path was too long by her reckoning. The bruises on her ribs and legs, where Nicholas and Nemec had caught her as she fell, throbbed. The cloth Joaquim had used to blindfold her was crushing her eyeballs. At every step, pain throbbed at the spot on her neck where Tanja's stick had landed. The room she was being roughly pushed into felt unpleasantly cold. Parquet creaked under her feet. Finally the procession stopped. There were whispers, surprised mutterings, and the shuffling of chairs.

"Who's this?"

Bianca pricked up her ears. It was a woman's voice—a soft voice she knew all too well. "Mrs. Catalon?"

She heard hurried footsteps, then the blindfold was removed. For a moment everything was blurry. They were still in the underground convent, but in a newer part. About fifty people were gathered in the room. It was brightly lit—a crystal chandelier hung from the ceiling above a large table of polished black stone. Documents lay scattered near a few computer screens. In the background Bianca could see huge bookcases that filled the entire wall. There they were: chronicles, antique books, files. Innumerable files. Mrs. Catalon gave Bianca a friendly smile, as if she had just invited her here for coffee.

"Bianca! What a coincidence. We were just talking about you."

There was renewed muttering.

"So that's her!" said an older man.

"The pair of them broke in," Joaquim's voice made itself heard.

Bianca looked over her shoulder. Apart from Joaquim and Tanja, only the other two Wolves were behind them. Tobias stepped forward and put Bianca's and Nicholas's cell phones, together with the map showing the floor plan, on the table.

"Who's the boy?" asked Mrs. Catalon.

Nicholas jumped when Tanja pulled down his blindfold. Nemec was standing not far from them, right beside the wolf, who was cowering at his feet, whimpering as he hid his eyes from the light. Jan was nowhere to be seen. Taken off, Bianca thought grimly. Oh well, at least he managed to get away.

"Klaus Jehle from the university magazine *Attempto.*" Nicholas introduced himself calmly.

"That's the name of the student who was at Mrs. Meyer's yesterday," a woman called out.

"Well, well, it's Mrs. Nyen," said Nicholas frostily. "Did you go out there all on your own to kill Mrs. Meyer? What did she do? Call you at the town archives and tell you she had Heinrich Feverlin's records?

A renewed muttering ran around the room. Mrs. Nyen went so pale that her wart stood out from her skin like a bluish-black boil. Gradually, Bianca began to recognize some of the other people standing in the room. And right at the back at the table sat—Sylvie. Her hand holding the pen still hovered over the paper half-filled with writing. Was she keeping minutes? The girl blanched and lowered her eyes. Beside the table stood a tall, balding man with round glasses—Dr. Almán, Joaquim's father.

"Nemec was going to take them to the northern exit with the wolf," said Tanja.

A groan ran through the crowd. Joaquim's father stepped out and dragged Nemec forward. The old janitor fell to his knees. The cut on his forehead that Joaquim had given him with his stick began to bleed again. Rage and panic were reflected in the onlookers' faces. Bianca thought the crowd was about to rush at Nemec and lynch him.

"What were you thinking?" roared Joaquim's father. The wolf-man ducked down and ran to Nemec.

"Stop!" cried Bianca.

The next moment she sank to the ground, groaning. Joaquim had hit her in the ribs with his stick.

"Shut up, Snow White," he said.

"Leave her alone!" Nicholas's face was distorted with rage. Tobias, Martin, and Tanja had to resort to all their fighting tricks to hold him back. It was not until Tobias hit Nicholas in the legs that they managed to force him to his knees.

"Put your weapons away," growled Dr. Almán. "And let go of him." Three sticks fell to the ground immediately; only Joaquim hesitated. The line of older Wolves eyed him threateningly.

"They broke in." Joaquim defended himself. "Into the old section! They were going to take the wolf away. The wolf!"

"Joaquim," warned Dr. Almán softly. Under the strict eye of his father Joaquim seemed to shrink. Finally he bent down and carefully laid his stick on the floor.

"Professor Wieser." Nicholas's voice rang out in the silence. An older man in a gray suit looked up. "And the gentlemen from pathology," Nicholas continued. "So you are involved in this too. No wonder Johanna Vargas's death was declared an accident."

The name that Nicholas had spoken hung in the air like an echo. From Sylvie's horrified face Bianca could tell what a serious error Nicholas had just made. In five quick paces the professor was beside him, seized the bonds around his hands, and jerked his arms up. "What else do you know?" asked Wieser. Nicholas groaned. Bianca screamed when she saw a knife gleam in the light.

"That's enough!" The words were not loud, but they were sharp. Wieser's hand froze in mid-air and then sank down. Everyone's eyes went to the door. Bianca blinked. All the Wolves—young and old—looked like children caught with their hand in the cookie jar. Bianca felt as if the ground were moving under her feet.

Marie-Claire Lalonde stepped into the silence, in full command. She was wearing a tailored dress reminiscent of a nun's habit. Her hip-length hair flowed loose over her shoulders, making her look astonishingly similar to the portrait of Belverina.

"Give me the knife," she ordered. The professor moved away from Nicholas and gave her the weapon, which she took with a nod. Behind her, Dr. Hasenberg appeared in the doorway. When he saw Bianca, he cursed. Madame went into the middle of the room, where Nemec and the wolf were sitting. With a graceful gesture she bent down to the janitor, lifting his chin with one hand. Nemec let her, his bound hands pressed painfully against his back.

"You were going to betray us and let the wolf go, Simon?" she said gently. "Why?"

Simon's eyelids trembled. "Because it's not right, Marie-Claire," he replied hoarsely. "A man's a man. I didn't understand for a long time—until you showed me what it's like to be locked up in here."

The headmistress sighed and stood up. "Oh, Simon!" She did not give the order to untie him, turning instead to Bianca. The Wolves watched in silence as Madame approached her and raised the knife. Strangely, Bianca was not afraid. The headmistress carefully cut through her bonds. Then she stepped in front of Bianca and gently took her face in her hands. Her smile was a little sad. Bianca swallowed. Against her will, she acknowledged how long she had been longing for this contact. At this moment she both hated and loved Madame.

"Why didn't you come to me?" asked the headmistress with gentle reproof. "I told you to come to me if you were ever worried."

Bianca turned away.

"But you were in Brussels," she said. Then she added scornfully, "And I thought..."

Madame Lalonde laughed.

"Yes, a lot of people think that. The alpha wolf is never the one that bites and threatens. The alpha wolf leads, and settles disputes. He only shows his teeth when necessary." With these words, she swung around and hit Joaquim straight in the face with all her strength. His head snapped back and then he doubled up. "Give me the fur," she whispered. Joaquim sniffled but stubbornly shook his head. In one purposeful stride, the headmistress was beside him, forcing him to the floor. He threw a pleading look at his father, but Mr. Almán folded his arms and did not move.

"That's against the rules," Joaquim gasped.

"José!" warned Madame.

Mr. Almán turned pale. The Wolves watched with bated breath. Even so, Bianca thought she saw an almost imperceptible movement. Finally, Dr. Hasenberg broke the silence.

"She isn't ready yet," he said.

"I'm still the one who decides that," the headmistress corrected him, sharply. "I know her better than any of you. Well?"

The teacher, the doctors, and Mrs. Nyen all went to stand at Madame's side. Dr. Almán and the young Wolves stayed back. Sylvie had not moved from her seat behind the table. Wide-eyed, she stared at Dr. Hasenberg, who was still standing between the two battle lines. The psychologist took a deep breath and closed his eyes for a moment.

"All right," he said finally, moving to Madame Lalonde's side. Dr. Almán's eyes flashed with rage. Reluctantly, he went over to his son, taking the wolf skin from his shoulders. Tanja and the other Wolves fell back. Bianca watched with horror as Madame took the wolf skin and held it out to her.

"It's meant to be yours. You found us and proved that you're better than he is. And I expected nothing else."

Suddenly Bianca realized why Joaquim and the Wolves hated her. Madame had made it clear from the start that Joaquim's days as chief of the young Wolves were numbered. Without being aware of it, from the very first day Bianca had been the intruder who was preferred above all of them and threatened Joaquim's status.

"I won't take the skin," she said.

Dr. Hasenberg laughed. The headmistress threw him an annoyed glance. "She'll take it," she answered. "I can feel it. She's like me when I was younger. And she's in better command of her thoughts than most other people here. When I ordered her to go, she was able to resist me. Me!" She stared at Bianca. "I called to her while she was sleeping, and she woke up and came to the window." Pictures began to form before Bianca's eyes. She had to blink. The phantom outside the window! So she hadn't been mistaken when she'd seen the nun's habit. "You were dreaming," whispered Madame's soft voice in her ear. "You saw the past. Only those of us with Belverina's gifts see the echoes of the past. You're one of us, Bianca."

"No!" shouted Bianca, pulling back. The older Wolves laughed.

"Oh, yes," Madame insisted. "All of us here are Belveriners —Belverina's children. Centuries ago, Maddalina, Hans Haber, and the other two prisoners escaped into the catacombs with their wolf. The children were driven away and scattered to the four corners of the earth. For many years Belverina's heirs lived here, underground, only going out at night to get food from the forest. That's how they survived. For decades now we've been trying to find the descendants of the witches' children. Over the generations they'd ended up all over the place. So we could find them more easily, we founded the Europa International School. And you, Bianca, are something special." She lowered her voice. "You're descended from Regina

Sängerin and from the wolf-man who lived within these walls in Maddalina's time."

Bianca felt as if there was not enough oxygen in the room. She was getting dizzy. "I'm not one of you," she cried. "You kill—and you keep human beings like animals!" She gestured toward the wolf-man.

"Let me explain," said Dr. Hasenberg, stepping forward. His manner was so kind and understanding that Bianca would have liked to spit in his face. She turned away in distaste. Nicholas turned his pale face toward her for a moment. She noticed that he was hunched forward and was hanging his head, as if he wanted to hide his face in the shadow of his hair. Bianca understood. Of course—he too was a descendant of the wolves.

"The order that existed centuries ago was Christian only in appearance," explained Dr. Hasenberg. "Belverina is our ancestor. She was never a Christian saint. She had the gift. Second sight. The power of suggestion, telepathy, and thought control. But people with special skills are soon betrayed. Her students and descendants learned from her tragic fate." Hasenberg raised his hands. "And what better place for wolves to hide than in the middle of a herd of sheep? No one would look for wolves, heathens, and thought controllers with the Lord's sheep." The Wolves murmured approvingly. "Belverina's heirs could set up their underground chambers and hide their true character in nuns' habits and gardeners' smocks, without fear of persecution or discovery. Their children were born down here, and this is where they learned to use their skills. They experimented with alchemy and magic and took, and still take today, the best from all the sciences. *Porta post portam*—we have managed to push open other doors behind the last door of the consciousness. And the journey is far from over. Of course, it isn't easy to find all their descendants. As I told you before, our ancestors also bequeath their fate to us. Even today there are many orphans among the descendants."

"Are all the students descendants of the Belveriners?" asked Bianca.

"Oh no," another man spoke. He seemed very familiar to Bianca. She remembered seeing his picture in the newspaper once. Of course—he was the mayor. "Among every thousand students there are three at the most who have the gift," he explained. "But that still doesn't mean that they can use it or are really suited to be accepted into our society." He gave a satisfied smile, seemingly very proud of being one of the chosen ones. "Maybe you've noticed the hypothetical questions in our application tests. They're intended to give us an idea of whether the student has this special intuitive talent. Those with the gift are not all necessarily descendants of the Belveriners, and they come from all over the world. It's our task to find them."

"But even the students without the gift are useful to us," Madame added. "We have a network of people who don't know our true mission. People who make a career for themselves and later are in the right place, people who make decisions."

"Like Caitlin?" asked Bianca. "Is she supposed to help you to recruit the next generation, when she's a teacher?

"Control the thoughts of others and you will control their deeds," Madame responded with a smile.

"You manipulate people!"

Madame Lalonde became serious. She bent forward so far that Bianca could see the dark ring around her iris. "Manipulate sounds like force," she whispered. "'Lead gently' is a better way of putting it. Who directs an arrow—you or your thoughts? You draw the bow, point the arrow in the right direction, and think of the target you'd like to hit. The thought counts, Bianca. Let's assume you could infiltrate the thoughts of an archer. He doesn't aim at the bull's eye; he aims to the side and loses the tournament. Then you'd have won, without trace, without cheating. Just using thoughts!"

"And then you can make him think of aiming at a person. Is that the perfect murder?" Bianca replied sharply.

"It's possible," replied Madame, smiling. "It's far harder to influence a person's thoughts in that direction. We're just beginning to understand this discipline, but we're working on it, believe me."

More pictures flooded Bianca's mind. She remembered how Nicholas had lied to her. Suddenly it was easy to hate him. Much too easy. Dazed, she wiped her eyes, and then another feeling won the upper hand: anger.

"Don't try that with me!" she hissed at Madame.

The headmistress laughed.

"You see: wolf sense. You have so much talent, Bianca. You should learn to use it."

"What about him?" The wolf-man was pressing closer to Simon Nemec.

"Our most important member," said Dr. Hasenberg. "He's everything to us—our medium, our focus, our confidante. Without him we're nothing. He's our memory, our soul. We are descended from the wolf—call him our totem, if you like."

"A highly civilized analysis, Professor Hasenberg," mocked Bianca. "And yet it comes from the mouth of a barbarian and murderer. You're all murderers!"

"We have to protect ourselves," replied Dr. Hasenberg icily. "Ourselves and our history—far too often other murderers have taken the lives of our wolves."

"And for that Johanna had to die?" cried Bianca. "She was one of you!" Scornfully she let her gaze roam over their faces. No one looked away. Only Sylvie looked down. "Perhaps Maddalina and the others were martyrs who fought for knowledge," Bianca continued. "But that doesn't justify anything you're doing today—anything at all! You're not the martyrs you pretend to be!"

Dr. Hasenberg's face was turning red and he was gasping for breath. He was about to say something, but Madame Lalonde stopped him with a wave of her hand.

"I don't approve of their killing Johanna," she explained. "It was an accident. Joaquim and the others..." her tone grew sharper "... discovered her by chance as she was trying to escape with the wolf through the exhibit room."

"We went down to prepare a little surprise for you in the museum. Joaquim and Tanja wanted to scare you," said Sylvie quietly, then fell silent again as Madame looked at her.

The headmistress continued. "A stick hit Johanna in the wrong place. The Wolves don't want to tell us who the mortal blow came from, and we respect their silence. Removing the wolf mark was an act of panic, too. But we don't expel anyone, right, Simon? In our society, mistakes happen—and we're there to protect each other."

"That's why you didn't come and get me for the test of courage," said Bianca to the Wolves. "You had to get Johanna out of the way. Were you going to hide her in Nemec's room until Madame decided what to do?"

"Yes, and we'd have managed it if you hadn't got in our way!" Tanja said resentfully.

"Why didn't you take her to the basement?"

"Because the door was shut," Sylvie replied for Tanja. "Johanna locked it behind her. We didn't know that she still had the key on her. We called Dr. Wieser and he told us to hide the body in the library—from there there's a passageway directly to the parking lot. He was going to pick her up during the night."

"You have a choice," said Madame gently, holding the wolf-skin out to Bianca again. "Accept your mission. We're not murderers—we offer people like Jan a chance, and Caitlin too—she comes from a poor family. We pay their scholarships and help children and young people all over the world." She lowered her voice even more. "Sadly, as always happens you're trying to do good, sometimes sacrifices have to be made. Would you condemn someone for panicking and shooting a burglar who's trying to kill his family? Johanna's death was an accident."

Bianca's gaze fell on Joaquim's unhappy face. His father, for whom he would never be good enough, had moved away from him. Bianca swallowed and looked straight at the headmistress. She was still Madame. Her Madame. There was a huge lump in her throat.

"If I decide to join you, what will happen to him?" she asked, pointing to Nicholas. "He knows everything now. Will you let him go?"

The threatening silence was answer enough. Bianca straightened her shoulders and took a step backward, her heart beating wildly.

"Mrs. Meyer's death was no accident," she said quietly. "The student didn't drown by accident. And no one deserves the fate of this boy. How barbaric do you have to be, to mutilate someone like that? I'll never be one of you, Marie-Claire. To me you're all murderers. And that includes you."

The scream was stifled, but Bianca still felt it ringing in her ears. The Wolves spun around. Simon Nemec was kneeling beside the wolf-man. His face was contorted with grief. Scraps of bandage and rope hung from his wrist. In his fist, which showed no sign of injury, he held Bianca's box cutter. As if in slow motion, blood ran down it and dripped onto the floor. Nemec's hoarse voice seemed to bounce off the walls.

"It must come to an end," he said to Marie-Claire. "And it has come to an end—now."

The wolf-man lay doubled up on the floor. Blood spread over the parquet.

"Run!" shouted Bianca to Nicholas. At the same moment Nemec raised his weapon again. Sylvie jumped up, and papers fluttered from the table. Nicholas and Bianca both rushed toward Nemec.

The bulbs in the crystal chandelier flickered. The next moment Bianca was standing in darkness as black as pitch. Her hands grasped the wolf-man's upper arm. With all her strength she tried to pull him up, but even just his arm was as heavy as lead. An elbow hit her jaw with full force. The arm slid out of her grasp, and the next moment she was swimming dazedly in a sea of bodies. There was a bang, then a dreadful splintering sound. Sparks flew as a computer monitor crashed onto the floor. Bianca rushed blindly into the darkness and stumbled over a stick lying on the floor. "Bianca?" The voice was right beside her. The next moment a lighter clicked on. The quivering light of the flame lit up Nicholas's face.

"He's dead!" cried Bianca. "We have to get out of here!"

Like a nightmare, Dr. Almán appeared in front of them. He swung with Joaquim's stick. Then the flame went out again. Somewhere there was a crackling sound. Bianca felt for the stick at her feet and grabbed it without thinking. Wood cracked. The blow left her hands numb.

"To the door!" she shouted at Nicholas. Hoping she would not hit Nicholas by mistake, she raised the stick and hit out again. Someone groaned. The chandelier flickered on again—two, three times. It seemed to Bianca that she was looking at innumerable disembodied images. One of them was of Dr. Almán, slowly getting back onto his feet. Another was of Sylvie grabbing Tanja's arms just as she was about to rush at Bianca.

"Go!" screamed Sylvie. Then the light went out with a final huge bang. Someone grabbed Bianca and dragged her toward the wall.

"Here, Nick!" called a voice. It was Jan! Bianca bumped into a door frame and groped her way outside. Panic-stricken cries and a crash reached into the hallway. There was the smell of burning plastic. Bianca looked around one last time—and immediately wished she had not. She saw flames slowly licking at the dry wood of a bookcase—and jumping to the dusty tomes. The old books burst into flame, the fire fed by the dust of many decades. The robe worn by one of the Wolves caught fire, and he rushed screaming into the middle of the crowd of people. Then all hell broke loose. Panic ensued, and people were stumbling around in confusion. Scraps of burning paper were floating down like red-hot rain. "Bianca!" Jan grabbed her roughly by the shoulder and swung her around, braced himself against the door, and slammed it shut. Almost blind in the sudden darkness, they stumbled through the passageway. Nicholas's lighter gave just enough light that they were able to duck in time to avoid hitting their heads on the stone roof of the passage where it dipped low. Without any way of orienting themselves, they stumbled through the passageways, got lost, and took side passages that sometimes looked familiar but were more often completely new to them. Again and again they heard cries and pounding footsteps. At one bend Jan recoiled and sniffed.

"Shit!" he whispered. "Something's burning here, too." Then his face brightened. "A draft!" He grabbed Nicholas's lighter and held it out in front of him. Bianca could see a fan as high as a man; it completely filled the end of the passage, creating suction as it turned. The lighter's flame flickered and went out. Jan's voice cracked.

"We're in a ventilation shaft!"

"Are we supposed to jump through the fan, one at a time?"

"Don't be stupid. There's always a maintenance passage around a fan."

Hand in hand they groped along the wall until Jan flicked on the lighter in the shelter of his hand. In front of them was a door with a big bolt. Together they pushed it open. Nicholas coughed. Smoke stung Bianca's eyes. Suction slammed the door behind them with a deafening thud.

After seemingly endless minutes Jan stopped again.

"A shaft and climbing irons," he cried. "Up we go!"

Bianca felt rusty metal. Coughing, she hauled herself hand over hand up the shaft. It must have been set at least 30 feet down into the ground. With his injured leg Nicholas took forever to make his way up. Bianca's hands were scraped and hurting when she finally saw light above her. Jan lifted up a grill, pushed it aside, and helped her, then finally Nicholas, to pull themselves over the smooth marble rim onto a stone floor. Panting, they fought for breath. Somewhere nearby, birds were twittering.

Dazed, Bianca opened her eyes and saw a chubby angel between cotton-wool clouds smiling down at her beatifically like a drunken man. Disbelievingly she blinked and raised her head. Hidden behind flower decorations and an altar, a railing rose up before them—and through a gothic gateway behind it they could see the early morning sky over the orphans' cemetery.

"We're in the Belverina chapel," Jan realized. "An airshaft that's classified as a historical monument. Very clever." He took Nicholas's bag, which he had been carrying the whole time, off his shoulder, stood up, and climbed over the railing. "Come on! Let's go! Let's not get caught again."

Cursing, Nicholas struggled to his feet. Bianca took his arm and pulled him along. Laboriously they hurried past the tombstones to the park. As she walked, Bianca glanced back and shuddered. The cemetery looked like the stage set for a cheesy horror film. Billowing smoke, rising from several graves and the chapel, began to cover the scene like fog. In the distance the siren of a fire engine wailed.

The first thing Bianca saw when the school was in sight was the glass of the library windows blowing out. Flames shot up into the sky, like a harbinger of the sun, which would soon rise. Students and teachers were crowding the entrance, pale with fright and freezing in T-shirts, dressing gowns, and pajamas. One of the fire engines pulling in braked so sharply that the gravel of the driveway sprayed up in all directions.

"How did you knock out the chandelier?" murmured Nicholas. Jan looked at him, wide-eyed.

"I didn't do anything to the chandelier," he said. "I'd only just found you when the lights went out." Suddenly he staggered. Bianca just caught him in time, and helped him sit down on the ground. His skin was cold from shock. "Maybe the bearing seized," he mumbled. "Then the motor overloaded. There was wood everywhere in the museum... But that can't be right. I'd built a fuse into it!"

"It wasn't you," said Bianca loudly. "The fire could have started for all sorts of reasons. There were candles burning down there—and I saw sparks when a monitor fell."

"But they may all be trapped!"

"You don't think there was only one entrance, do you?" asked Nicholas bleakly.

BELVERINA'S DESCENDANTS

COLIN SINCLAIR HAD NOT HAD TIME for a shower. Unshaven, he sat facing Bianca, looking at the prints of Nicholas's digital photos.

"OK, then. You were doing research for a history essay for Mrs. Meyer and discovered that someone had forged the record of the witch trial. That much I understand. But what does that have to do with the fire?"

"No idea," replied Bianca. "I've told you everything I know."

Sinclair looked at her suspiciously and wrinkled his brow. "Now why don't I quite believe you?" He sighed deeply and took another gulp of coffee. "You're obliged to answer my questions—you do know that, I hope?" he said rather more severely.

Bianca nodded.

"It must have been a very unusual fire," continued Detective Sinclair. "Or there were accelerants involved. We found a tamper-proof lock on the museum door."

"They said that on the news today, yes," replied Bianca softly. At the thought of the panic in the assembly room, of the screams and faces, she felt sick again from grief and horror.

Sinclair nodded and ran his hands through his hair, agitated.

"OK. You have my card?"

"No. Madame Lalonde didn't give it to me last time."

He looked at her for so long that she began to feel uncomfortable. Finally he reached into a drawer and took out a card. After a moment's consideration he picked up a pen and scribbled a number on the back.

"My cell number. You can call me anytime, if you think of anything else."

Bianca nodded and attempted a smile. She found it hard. Sylvie's face swam before her eyes. She could not hold back her tears. Detective Sinclair took a box of tissues from the drawer and handed it to her without a word. He waited until she was in control again.

"I have a question for you, Detective Sinclair," she said softly. "I noticed in the town museum that you donated to the orphans' cemetery. Why?"

She had managed to catch him by surprise. To her astonishment he seemed embarrassed.

"It was my grandmother's wish. After the war she and my grandfather used to meet in the park by the cemetery. It meant a lot to her. And when she died, I donated part of what I inherited toward the restoration." His smile grew bitter. "Hmm. If I'd known I was financing the secret passages and air shafts of a cult..." He looked up at her quickly. "Did you know?"

"No."

He made a dismissive gesture, giving up at last. "OK, OK. Well then..." Slowly he stood up, reaching out to shake her hand. "I don't imagine we'll see each other again very soon. But I expect you're staying in town."

NICHOLAS AND JAN WERE ALREADY WAITING in La Bête. The café was deserted, the tourists preferring to head out to the ruin of the school and to the orphans' cemetery to compete with the international news stations for a spectacular photo of the salvage operations.

"So?" asked Nicholas without even greeting her first.

Bianca sank into a chair and shook her head. "I don't think he's one of them."

The relief left Nicholas's expression soft and a little sad. Shock was still evident in his face. Bianca took hold of his hand under the table.

"Let's wait and see what Sinclair does with the information," said Jan, his voice rough. "I don't trust anyone in this town, anyway. I'm leaving."

"You're going home?"

"What would I do there? No, I'm taking off. The last thing I need now is having my name appear in some police report." Nervously he drummed on the table with his fingers. His cheeks were hollow and the deep rings under his eyes made him look older. The carefree, cool Jan had disappeared. "Caitlin said I should take the next plane to Dublin, but I think it will be better to hitchhike. And maybe I can do odd jobs along the way to pay for the ferry."

"You've spoken to Caitlin?" cried Bianca. "My mother was quite hysterical because she had called asking for me at home."

"I haven't actually spoken to her. Her family has just moved to Dublin and doesn't have a phone yet. And the Wolves had stolen her cell phone. That's why we couldn't contact her. But I just got an email from her. She's at the end of her tether. But she's not the only one." He patted the side pocket of his jacket. "I'm dying to see what she says when she sees her final exam."

"But it won't be any use to her any more," murmured Nicholas.

"Caitlin can ace any exam—at any school," replied Jan.

"Did you tell her everything?" asked Bianca.

"Absolutely not," said Jan with emphasis. "That's your business." He stood up, rapped on the table in farewell, and left. They watched him through the café window as he went across the market place, shoulders hunched, toward the main street. Directly in front of the central pillar stood a TV news team, asking passers-by for their comments. An old man was waving his hands dramatically. Bianca had the feeling she was watching the mime-show of a great tragedy.

"Our story," said Nicholas despondently. He put his mother's bag on the table and took out the records that they had rescued from Hasenberg's office.

"Your story." He pushed a genealogical chart over to Bianca. "'ba'—that's your abbreviation. And here's your ancestral line, back to the wolf-man." With a bitter undertone he added, "Belverina's heirs. At least we both know now where we come from." Bianca studied the symbols and lines. Right at the bottom, Hasenberg had noted down the profession the Wolves had intended for Bianca. "Neurologist," she read out. "And I'll bet they'd have managed it. I'd have spent my life researching brain waves and engrams."

Carefully she smoothed the paper. There were the names of her biological parents. Both had died on the same day, a year after Bianca's birth. Strangely, the thought of her mother—her mother wearing her hotel uniform—moved her much more.

For the first time in months she could think of the word "home" without it sounding false and bitter. Nicholas gave her a sideways glance.

"What?"

"Admit it. In the assembly room you believed Marie-Claire for a moment."

She lowered her gaze. "Only for a moment. She was really convinced about what she was doing. She believed she was a good person!"

"You miss her, don't you?"

Bianca was silent.

"No more secrets," warned Nicholas softly. "We promised each other that."

She had to clear her throat to speak. "I liked her." It was not the whole truth.

Nicholas looked away and surveyed the big town hall clock. Bianca was still amazed that time was marching on as if the night before had never happened. Through the open door the wind carried the TV interviews into the café. And there was something else—was that breathing? The hairs on Bianca's neck stood up—was someone standing right behind her? She looked around, but no one was there.

"What's up?" Nicholas looked at her in concern.

"Nothing," she said quickly.

I'm just imagining it, she thought, trying to reassure herself. It's echoes. Just echoes!

"I'm so sorry about Johanna," she whispered, turning her focus back to Nicholas. "And about your brother."

"History repeats itself," said Nicholas huskily. "When the totem dies or leaves the convent, the Wolves die, too." His hands shook as he pushed his hair back from his face. "I still can't believe I had a brother," he whispered. "I never knew—all those years!"

Suddenly he took Bianca into his arms and rested his forehead on her shoulder. It felt incredibly good to have him so close. "I'll tell you something," he said. "I don't believe he's dead."

"Stop!" Bianca pleaded. She turned her head and looked into Nicholas's eyes. "I touched him—he didn't move. He gave no sign of life."

Nicholas's voice grew even quieter. "He was gone. When the light flickered on, he wasn't lying where he'd fallen. Maybe he was just injured and unconscious?"

"Even if he wasn't in the same place—what does that prove? The others dragged him away. Or your view of his body was blocked. After all, we didn't even know where in the room we were!"

His arms around her eased, telling her that he was beginning to relax.

"You're probably right," he said. "But I keep thinking about it. There were other exits, weren't there?"

"I can't say, Nicholas. The floor plan only showed the old section of the underground building."

"But if there were... other exits. Do you realize what that would mean for us?"

Bianca looked at her hands and fought against the feeling that the firm ground, which she had only just stepped onto, was beginning to shake again. Red! She struggled to breathe, terrified. Her heart was racing. For a strange moment she saw her hands—and yet not her hands: snow-white skin and a dark-red patch of dried blood. Only when she blinked did the vision disappear. Stay calm, she told herself. It doesn't have to mean anything.

And yet—in her mind she had an almost physical sensation of touching.

"It would mean that those who survived would look for us." Nicholas had answered his own question. "We'd never be safe. Not anywhere."

For a long time they sat in silence, both listening to the echoes of their own story.

"Three dead bodies have been identified so far." The TV journalist spoke into the camera. "Marie-Claire Lalonde, the headmistress of the Europa International School, José Almán, the chairman of the board of the Maddalina of Trenta Foundation, and Dr. Robert Conrad, the town's mayor. But other teachers at the school and professors from the university are suspected of being members of the supposed cult as well. Because of extent of the destruction, it is not possible to say at this time how many people have perished in the catacombs. The recovery work continues. It's assumed that at least..."

"Hi!" someone called out to the two of them, "Can I ask you two a couple of questions?" Startled, they looked up. A young man stood in front of them holding a microphone. "I'm from *Attempto,* and I'm doing a piece on the Maddalina of Trenta case. What do you think..."

"Nothing at all," said Bianca, pulling Nicholas up from his chair. "We're not from around here."

EPILOGUE

RED! IT WOKE UP TREMBLING. In Its whole body It felt fear, fear that was crawling over Its limbs leaving a slimy trail, like the cluster of snails that It had once eaten and about which It still dreamed sometimes. With a jerk It raised Its head and sniffed the air. Looking at the colors hurt—a hundred different kinds of green, brown, and wet black in the much-too-bright light at the cave's entrance. And again and again the red of Its thoughts—the glowing, red-hot, roaring thing It had escaped from. The voices and noises still resounded painfully in Its ears—screams and splintering noises, and the snarling of fearful thoughts that had flooded through It. In Its memory they became so loud that It howled in fright. It bared Its teeth and crawled back even deeper into Its refuge. The cave smelled of moss and bark, and its stones felt good—familiar and safe. Its fresh wound, struck by the strong Other's sharp tooth, was hurting. And then there was another image. "Come!" said the gentle voice. It had lost her, but somewhere, in the distant shadow of Its own thoughts, It felt her gentle presence, quite near. Comforted, It closed Its eyes.

It was not until much later, when the painful colors had turned into comforting gray shadows, that It crawled outside, cowering down in fear. The air around It moved like a living being and It cried out in anguish. But then It sniffed the air and dared to take Its first step. The distance, the quietness, were frightening, and yet something in It began to stir. Nobody called It back, nobody was there to lead It or drive It forward. No strange thoughts disturbed Its peace. Only the shadows and a multitude of unfamiliar smells, seductive and frightening at the same time. Its steps got faster and faster. Soft, feathery undergrowth, like wet fur, flew under Its feet. Its heart beat wildly, and yet It did not feel tired any more, just a strange, blazing intoxication. The last remnants of fear disappeared, and the pain in Its wounds only pulsed dully, like a dim memory. The distance bore It like a gentle hand across the ground.

And It ran.

It ran.

ABOUT THE AUTHOR

NINA BLAZON is the award-winning author of several historical and fantasy novels. She won the Wolfgang Hohlbein Prize for her first fantasy novel, *Under The Curse.* She lives in Stuttgart, Germany.